"Having second t

Dani glanced up, the gr   making her catch her breath.

Oh, boy. She was in more trouble than she'd initially thought.

"Nope." She ripped her attention away from him and focused on Jaxon and the girls as they chased each other across the field. "I'm happy to help."

"So you say." Mac's grin grew. He glanced at his kids before leaning in to whisper, "But my girls can be a handful."

She smiled and tapped his chest with a finger. "I can be a handful myself, in case you haven't noticed."

His laughter faded and he studied her from head to toe. "Oh, I've noticed."

He shifted closer, his fingers caressing her elbow.

"What're y'all whispering about?"

They sprang apart. Maddie stood a couple of feet behind Mac, frowning, and waiting for an answer. Nadine and Jaxon stood at their sister's side with smug grins.

"Nothing." Dani stumbled back.

Oh yeah. She was definitely in over her head.

Dear Reader,

Writers deal with thousands of words on a daily basis. We weigh syllables to create the right rhythm, sift through phrases to find those with the most impact and scrutinize words we've typed for hours, trying our best to decide which ones to cut and which ones to save.

Over time, a few have become my favorites. One, in particular.

Home.

There's something about it that warms my heart and helps me breathe easier. Something simple and precious. Something that has little to do with bricks or shingles and so much to do with the people I love and admire. Because that's how those people make me feel. Warm and welcome. Valued and forgiven. There's no greater home in the world than the one you find in someone who has seen you at your worst...but still loves you just as much as when you're at your best.

In A *Home with the Rancher*, Dani Vaughn wants to be seen. To be noticed and loved. And Mac Tenley has been searching for home for a long time. What they find in each other is more than either ever expected.

As always, thank you for reading.

April

A HOME WITH THE RANCHER

—

APRIL ARRINGTON

HARLEQUIN® WESTERN ROMANCE

Recycling programs
for this product may
not exist in your area.

ISBN-13: 978-1-335-69961-9

A Home with the Rancher

Copyright © 2018 by April Standard

Printed in U.S.A.

April Arrington grew up in a small Southern town and developed a love for movies and books at an early age. Emotionally moving stories have always held a special place in her heart. April enjoys collecting pottery and soaking up the Georgia sun on her front porch.

Visit April at Twitter.com/april_arrington or Facebook.com/authoraprilarrington.

Books by April Arrington

Harlequin Western Romance

Men of Raintree Ranch

Twins for the Bull Rider
The Rancher's Wife
The Bull Rider's Cowgirl
The Rancher's Miracle Baby

Visit the Author Profile page
at Harlequin.com for more titles.

Dedicated to Billie Ann

Doesn't matter where we are...
Sharing laughs on the day job,
gossiping over cheese sticks in a
restaurant or kicking back in a cool
movie theater on a hot summer day.
With you, every place feels like home.

You're more than a coworker
or friend—you're family.

And I thank my lucky stars
God put us on the same path.

Chapter One

Lies always multiplied. That was one reason Danielle Vaughn never told them.

"I said what's your name, ma'am?"

Danielle eyed the older man straddling the wooden fence and cringed, wondering how big this lie would get. At the moment, it stuck in her throat, feeling sharper and thicker than the angular mountains shrouded in dense fog at the man's back. And it beat heavier through her veins than the rhythmic pound of a hammer in the distance.

He scoffed and the straw of hay clenched between his teeth flopped against his scruffy jaw. "You got one, don't you, gal?"

"Danielle Vau—" She bit her tongue and winced. *Jones.* That was the one she'd settled on. Her lips trembled. *Wasn't it?* "Danielle Jones. I'm here to see Mac Tenley."

The man's expression remained bored and he looked away, chewing on the hay and shifting to a more comfortable position on the top fence rung. "Mac's busy. Whatcha want with him?"

His land. Or rather, her father wanted it. Danielle swallowed hard against the churn in her stomach. Despite his dismissive laughter and her misgivings, she'd promised to acquire it for him.

She glanced up at the sign hanging over the entrance of the gravel driveway, the words *Elk Valley Ranch* barely discernable on the weathered wood. Judging from first impressions and the photos she'd seen in the New York boardroom of Vaughn Real Estate, the guest lodge and cabins that lay beyond the winding drive would need a ton of work.

"My name is Danielle," she repeated, returning her eyes to the man. "But I go by Dani."

He stilled, his wrinkled brow furrowing as he faced her. "*Dani* Jones?"

She nodded.

His eyes narrowed then traveled down the length of her. His jaw slackened, the hay falling out of his mouth and his loud guffaws echoing across the peaceful Tennessee landscape. "Hey, Tim! Get a load of this."

Dani stiffened.

The distant pounding stopped and moments later, a younger man rounded the bend in the driveway, carrying a hammer and frowning. "You think you could do at least ten minutes of work today, man?"

"Aw, forget that, Tim." The man jumped off the fence, jabbed a thick finger in her direction then doubled over with laughter. "This puny girl here's the *man* Mac said was coming to interview as new hand."

Puny? Girl? Dani's face heated and she gritted her teeth, wishing she wore her stilettos instead of flat-soled sneakers. She'd shove the sharp edge right up his chauvinistic—

"Mac's gonna…" The man sucked in quick breaths between bouts of laughter. "Mac's gonna have a fit."

"I hate to spoil a boy's good time." Dani edged around the chuckling buffoon and extended her hand. "So I'll just ask a man for assistance instead." She smiled. "Tim, was it? I'm Dani. It's nice to meet you and I'm sure it'll be even nicer working with you since it's obvious your help is lacking." She jerked her chin over her shoulder as the man stopped laughing. "Would you please tell me where I can find Mac Tenley?"

Tim grinned, his handsome face lighting with amusement. "Yes, ma'am." He took her hand, squeezed gently then pointed toward the lush line of poplar and cedar trees obscuring the winding driveway. "Just follow the drive up to the lodge and go on in. The office opened a half hour ago and Mac's probably still in there."

"Thank you."

Tim's grin widened and he tipped his Stetson. "Look forward to working with you."

Dani nodded, her smile faltering at the kind gleam in his eyes. It was one thing to think up a lie and rehearse it in your head. It was quite another to actually tell it. Especially to an honest, hardworking man like Tim.

She returned to the battered compact car she'd parked at the ranch's entrance, her lip curling as she passed the lazy cowboy standing by the fence.

That fool she had no qualms about deceiving.

He scowled and muttered under his breath, eyes dark with disdain.

Ignoring him, Dani opened the creaky door and slid behind the wheel. A few quick twists of her wrist and the engine sputtered to life then groaned its way up the graveled path. She pushed her foot harder on the pedal and held her breath, doubting the pitiful contraption would creep its way up the steep hill. A glance in the rearview mirror proved the two men staring behind her had their doubts, too.

"Focus," she muttered, leaning forward and tightening her grip on the steering wheel. "Keep your head up and your eyes open."

And what spectacular scenery there was for a pair of open eyes. Once she cleared the enormous hill and passed through the dense woods, the land opened up, sprawling in all directions and stretching lazily into the foothills of the Smoky Mountains. The summer sun tinged the mountain fog with rosy undertones and bathed the green valley in golden light.

"Beautiful," she whispered.

That was an understatement. She shook her head and rolled down the window, unable to find the words for it. The sweet, clean air of Elk Valley made the remembered feel of thick wind whipping across busy New York streets seem stifling. And the leisurely hum of wildlife rustling through the trees, the sight of birds flapping in the breeze and the sound of horses whinnying in the distance were even more cajoling.

The valley seduced her senses, beckoning her to stop the car, collapse in the wide field like a child and roll across the thick tufts of grass for days. Fold her arms behind her head, stare at the blue sky and dream of being more than she was.

She laughed. What would the elite New York socialites she rubbed shoulders with say about such an immature, impulsive thought? Her laughter trailed away. Exactly what they'd always said, probably. That she was behaving like an uncouth tomboy instead of a twenty-seven-year-old woman.

Or worse. They might suggest the same thing her father and younger brother had. That, like her late mother, she was better suited for shopping, decorating and organizing charity events rather than running a business. Especially, a multi-million-dollar one like her father's thriving real estate firm.

Your brother will make a better vice-president.

Because he's a man. Her father had said it without saying it. The look on his face had affirmed her suspicions and the gentle tone of his voice revealed his reluctance at having to spell it out for her. Then she'd been relegated to the back seat, signing paperwork and looking pretty for powerful male clients. Activities she detested and a game she refused to play any longer.

Dani winced. She'd always disappointed him. That was how it'd been ever since she was born a girl instead of the strapping son her father had expected.

It was ridiculous, really. This undying need to prove herself to him. Or any man, for that matter.

She tensed her stomach muscles, trying to still the waves of nausea rising within her. The entire endeavor—including this charade—made her sick. Sick of feeling like she'd never fit in or measured up. Sick of her weaknesses and herself.

Dani straightened, maneuvered the troubled car around the final curve in the driveway and brought it to a sputtering halt at the end. There was one thing her father understood and appreciated more than anything. And it never failed to capture his attention—or approval.

Money. The largest sum of which resided in the untapped potential of this awe-inspiring valley. Magnificent acres of land his employees had failed to persuade the owner, Mac Tenley, to sell.

"If a man can't get the job done," she chimed, shoving the door open and rising to her feet, "send in a woman."

Dani smiled and looked up, taking in the massive log lodge in front of her. "You might not want to sell now, Mac Tenley. But you will."

She'd make sure of it. That was why she'd applied online for the only available—and shockingly low-paying—position on the ranch. Working as a ranch hand for a few weeks would give her access to the lodge and cabins. A feat her younger brother hadn't been able to manage. Of course, her father and brother didn't know about this aspect of her plan—they thought she'd come out here for an extended sales pitch. Which, to be fair, was her ultimate goal. After scoping the lay of the land and drawing up plans for what could be the highest-grossing luxury retreat in Elk Valley, Tennessee, she'd show Mac Tenley the benefits of selling and make a more than fair offer.

She'd heard he was a tough customer. A greedy one, in fact. So she'd throw in a few perks to sweeten the deal. This land was valuable and she'd pay him what it was worth and then some. Enough to turn any money-grubbing head—even if she had to dig into her savings.

Her father would be happy, Mac Tenley would be happy and she'd be happy. It'd be a winning situation for them all.

Confidence renewed, Dani snagged a worn duffel bag from the back seat and hoisted the strap over her shoulder. The bulky buckle dug into her flesh then loosened with a sharp pop.

"Shoot." Her hands shot out and lifted the bag to ease the weight off the flimsy strap.

Seemed she'd overdone it in the disguise department. She should've known the old putter car behind her was a bad choice when the used car salesman had tried to talk her out of it. And it didn't look as though the bag would make it through more than one day.

She'd been aiming to look broke. Instead, she was pretty sure she looked destitute.

No matter. If it meant a better chance of keeping the job as a ranch hand and gaining access to the property, all the better.

She made the long walk up the stone path past an empty fire pit then up a steep set of stairs. The porch was wide, lined with large windows and, though in desperate need of more seating, had an absolutely stunning view of the green valley and surrounding mountains.

The foyer was even more impressive. A wide room with hardwood floors and a stone fireplace served as a reception and lounge area. Multiple seating areas were arranged in a welcoming fashion around the room but the chairs looked worn and stiff with only two couples occupying them. Judging from the disgruntled looks on their faces, they wouldn't remain there for much longer.

A sharp scream cut through the silent waiting area. Dani jumped and a second stitch popped on her bag.

"Nadine Tenley." Several thuds and a breathless, feminine voice came from the direction of the empty reception desk on the other side of the room. "If you don't cut that out—"

"That hurts and my hair don't need brushing." A second voice. Higher-pitched and much younger sounding. "Why can't I go hiking? It's not fair. Maddie and me don't get to do nothing just cuz we're girls."

"I don't think Maddie wants to do anything with you right now seeing as how you've made her cry."

"Ain't nobody made her cry. She done that all on her own." A sigh. "I'm sorry, Ms. Ann, but it just ain't fair."

"Excuse me." Dani approached the counter then hesitated, peeking over the top as a phone began ringing on the desk. "I'm looking for Mac Tenley. I have an appointment but I'm early. Is he available?"

More thuds then a gray head appeared as a woman straightened, placed a pink comb on the counter and smiled. It was strained. "Good morning. Welcome to Elk Valley Ranch." She smoothed a shaky hand over her disheveled hair and glanced at the ringing phone. "May I have your name, please?"

"Dani Jones. I'm here for an interview."

The receptionist was jostled, fell against the counter then uttered a tsk. A small child—*around seven years old?*—darted out then skidded to a halt at the toes of Dani's cheap sneakers.

"An interview?" The little girl blinked wide green eyes up at her, her tangled blond hair sticking out at odd angles. Her jeans and T-shirt were muddy and rumpled. "You the new hand my daddy's gonna hire?"

Daddy? Dani frowned, mentally sifting through the facts she'd gathered on Mac Tenley. Twenty-nine, owner of Elk Valley Ranch and single. There'd been no mention of a wife or children. And certainly no mention of the cute spitfire in front of her.

"I—"

"Nadine, apologize to your sister right now."

Dani stilled, the low rumble sending a delicious

shiver over her skin. She glanced up…then up a smidge more. A tall, muscular man with rumpled blond hair and dark green eyes strode down a narrow side-hallway, carrying a young girl. He smoothed a big hand over the girl's curls as she buried her face in his neck.

Nadine spun, propped her hands on her hips and raised her voice over the shrill clang of the phone. "What'd I do?"

The second girl lifted her head and rubbed at her tear-stained cheeks. "You know what you did." She was a perfect replica of Nadine except for freshly combed hair, pink ribbons and a flowery sundress. "You called me a sissy."

Nadine shrugged. "Well, you were kinda acting like one."

"That's enough." The man shot a stern look at Nadine then glanced over his shoulder. "Ms. Ann, would you please answer the phone?"

Ann held up her hands and blew out a breath. "Yes, I'm just all out of sorts. I'm sorry, Mac, but I'm not a babysitter. Your father never asked me to watch after children while I ran the front desk."

He grimaced. "I know and I apologize. It won't happen again."

Dani pulled in a sharp breath and held it. So this was Mac Tenley. Twenty-nine, owner of Elk Valley Ranch and a…*daddy*. Her lungs burned. Definitely not what she'd expected. Or planned for. Deceiving a man was bad enough but lying to children? Her heart slammed against her ribs. There was no way she could go through with this. She'd just have to return to New York and come up with a new strategy.

A bell rang and warm air wafted through the room. Dani turned, watching as one of the couples exited.

"I'm sorry, were you waiting for a room?"

Dani spun back to find Mac studying her. She opened her mouth, releasing the pent-up breath, and tried not to stare at his wide chest, broad shoulders and sensual lips.

His strong jaw firmed. His gaze roved over her face then lingered on her mouth, heating her cheeks.

"It's a girl, Dad," Nadine piped, tugging at his jeans.

Mac started then jerked his eyes back up to meet hers.

"I can see that." He bent, set the second girl on her feet then nodded. "I'm Mac Tenley, owner. Sorry about the wait. Ms. Ann will check you in momentarily. If you'll excuse me?"

Dani sighed as he moved past her and made his way over to the sole couple still in the waiting area. *Time to go.* She tightened her grip on her bag and started toward the exit.

"Are you gonna shovel the horse poop?" Nadine asked, skipping in front of her. "Cuz we hate when dad makes us shovel the poop. We usually have to do it when we get in trouble."

The other girl scooted to her sister's side, tears gone and interest sparking in her eyes. "Who's she?"

"The new hand," Nadine said.

"But she's not a cowboy like Mr. Tim."

"I know." Nadine lifted her chin, a self-satisfied grin appearing. "She's a girl."

The child looked Dani over then stepped forward and held out her hand. "Hello. I'm Maddie."

Unable to resist, Dani smiled and shook her hand. "Dani. It's nice to meet you."

"Girls, I asked you to stay put in the game room," Mac muttered as he walked by. He escorted the couple from the waiting area to the front desk and smiled. "I apologize for the wait. Ms. Ann will have you settled in no time and the first night will be free. I hope you enjoy your stay and if you need anything, please don't hesitate to ask."

The couple thanked him and Ann began checking them in. Mac took both girls by the hand then started leading them down the hall.

"But, Dad, wait." Nadine jerked against Mac's hold, halting him. "That's the new hand you said was coming."

Dani bit her lip and headed for the door.

"What?"

Mac's sexy voice echoed across the foyer. Dani quickened her step.

"The new *hand*," Nadine repeated. "Dani Jones."

Dani twisted the doorknob, goose bumps breaking out on her nape as Mac's rumble drew closer.

"Wait. Are you Dani Jones?"

Dani's hand froze around the doorknob. This was it. Time to end it. No more lies. She didn't have to say she was Dani Jones. She'd just say she'd made a mistake. That after seeing the state of the place, she'd decided the job wasn't for her and then she'd leave.

And that'd be the end of it.

She glanced over her shoulder as his intense gaze traveled from the top of her head to the tips of her shoes.

"I don't mean to be rude," Mac said. "But you're not what I was expecting."

Dani frowned. The disappointment in his dark eyes raised familiar hackles. Ones that stiffened her back and clenched her jaw every time her brother shut her out of a business meeting or her father asked her to file another stack of paperwork.

Her mouth opened, the curt words jumping off her tongue before she had a chance to stop them. "Why? Because I'm a woman?"

DAMN. HE'D WALKED right into that one.

Mac winced, taking in the angry flare of the woman's mesmerizing blue eyes and tight set of her slim shoulders. He shook his head and held up a hand. "Now, that's not what I meant."

Though it hit closer to the truth than he wanted to admit. He sure hadn't pictured a woman when he'd finally received an email in response to his ad a week ago. And he'd assumed the odd spelling of Danny—with an *i*—had simply been unfamiliar to him. It'd never occurred to him that a woman was applying for the job.

Of course, seeing as how he was strapped for cash and in desperate need of extra help, he'd had no problem overlooking the applicant's lack of experience when he'd read the email. If this Dani was willing to accept the next-to-nothing pay balanced out with free lodging and meals, Mac was more than eager to hire him.

Her. Mac shifted from one boot to the other and cleared his throat. He'd be more than eager to...

She faced him, adjusted the strap on her shoulder

then put her hands on her hips. The action pulled her thin T-shirt tight across her ample breasts and the firm tap of her sneaker on the hardwood floor drew his eyes to the shapely length of her jean-clad legs.

"Well?" she asked, the soft curves of her mouth tightening into a hard line. "What *did* you mean?"

Ah, hell. He tore his gaze away from the appealing curves of her hips, refocused on her face and ignored the latent heat stirring in his blood. Add ogling to employment discrimination.

Figured the first woman in four years that sucker-punched him with lust would be a potential employee. He didn't have time for women and kept his distance from them for a reason. He grimaced. Three reasons, actually. But it looked like fate was hell-bent on making his life difficult.

"I just meant that I was expecting someone different."

Her eyes narrowed, her thick lashes obscuring those beautiful blues. "A man, I suppose?"

Mac glanced down at his girls, each hugging one of his legs. They stared up at him. Innocent curiosity lifted Maddie's expression. Nadine's judgmental scowl—which she flashed him often lately—deepened.

Cringing, he looked up. "You have to admit, your name can be misleading."

She flushed and the redness stamping her face spread down the graceful curve of her neck.

"You are Dani Jones, aren't you?" He placed a hand on the girls' shoulders and hugged them closer.

She'd never actually confirmed it and the heat in his blood cooled, slowing it in his veins and leading him to scrutinize her more closely. Her clothing had seen better days and the ragged shoes she sported wouldn't last more than a week on the ranch. But her nails, which still pressed into her hips, were manicured to perfection. The soft shade of pink nail polish matched the lipstick accentuating her lush mouth and the stud gemstones in her delicate earlobes.

Every bit of which screamed the exact opposite of a hard-living, nomadic ranch hand who'd applied for the position.

"Look," Mac scoffed. "If you're not Dani Jones and some developer sent you out here to sweet-talk me into selling my land, you might as well sashay back to where you came from. I've had at least seven agents here this week already and I'm not in the mood for another debate. I'm not interested in selling my land. I'm interested in hiring help."

"But she *is* Dani Jones," Nadine said, frowning up at him. "That's what she said. And a girl can be a ranch hand if she wants to." She released his leg, walked over to the woman and grabbed her hand. "Tell him. A girl can be a ranch hand, can't she?"

The redness marring the woman's fair skin deepened as she looked down at Nadine. Hesitating, she licked her lips then smiled, saying softly, "Yes. A girl can do anything she sets her mind to." She faced him head-on. "I'm not here to sweet-talk you and I'm not prone to sashaying anywhere. I'm here to work. And yes, I'm... Dani."

Mac sighed. Well. That eased one of his worries but it sure didn't do much for the others.

He reached out, tugged Nadine back to his side then nodded at Dani. "You might not like what I've got to say but I'm gonna be honest with you because that's the only way I operate." The wary look on her face caused his skin to prickle with unease. "I'd hire you as easily as I would any man so long as I knew you could get the job done." He reassessed her slight build and slender arms. "The pay isn't much and the hours are long. The work is also physically demanding. Anyone I hire would have to be able to lift at least fifty pounds without breaking a sweat."

She straightened. "I'm aware of all that. And I'm tougher than I look."

"Do you have any horseback-riding experience?"

"A little."

"A little?" He frowned. "What's that mean?"

She looked away. "I've ridden once or twice." A sheepish look crossed her face. "A few years ago."

Mac rubbed the tight knot at the back of his neck. "What about watering and feeding horses? Cleaning stalls?"

She shook her head.

"I suppose you have no experience haying or fencing, either?"

More headshaking. Lord, help him. Forget inexperienced. She was the epitome of green.

Nadine jerked on his jeans pocket and whispered, "I can teach her the scooping poop part, Dad."

Maddie pulled on his shirt, her pink hair ribbon falling over her cheek. "And I can show her the watering part."

Mac forced a smile, tugged the twins off his legs and nudged them toward the hallway. "Girls, I need to show Ms. Dani around. You'll have to wait here." Nadine grumbled under her breath and Maddie made a soft sound of disappointment. "Why don't y'all stay with Ms. Ann..."

A look of trepidation crossed Ann's face. She eyed the girls then backed further behind the desk, her hands clutching papers and a stapler to her chest.

"Well..." *Hell.* How was he supposed to watch his girls, school a new employee *and* finish the twelve hours of work already lined up for the day? Mac scraped a hand through his hair. "I guess you can come with us."

"Yes!" Nadine pumped a small fist in the air.

Maddie smiled. "Okay, Daddy."

He shook his head as the girls pushed past him and ran to Dani's side. "Now, look. There'll be no misbehaving." He pointed a finger at the girls and frowned. Man, he sounded just like an uptight, run-down dad. Which, he had to admit, was exactly how he felt. "No disobeying me. And no wandering off."

"Yes, sir." Nadine's angelic grin twitched devilishly at the corners.

Warmth flooded Mac's chest and he stifled a laugh. These pint-sized blondes had wrapped him around their little fingers the day they were born. And he didn't mind it a bit. Though he didn't spend a fraction of the amount of time he should with them nowadays.

He frowned and studied the scuff marks on the hardwood floor. Or his son, for that matter. It'd been ages since he'd been able to spend a day with any of his three children. What kind of father did that make him?

Mac tensed. *A bad one.* But this past week, he'd actually managed to get ahead of chores. And hiring an extra hand would ease some of his load, giving him a chance to be a decent father for a change.

Clearing his throat, he reached around Dani and opened the door. "After you."

A soft breeze drifted in, ruffling through her long, brown hair and carrying the sweet scent of her shampoo to his nostrils. His fingers tingled. He balled his fist, shaking off the unwelcome urge to touch the shiny strands.

She glanced up, that soft mouth parting on a swift intake of air. "Thank you."

He led her down the stairs and up the stone path to the driveway then across the grounds. She kept pace with him, listening and watching carefully as he pointed out the various sections of the lodge. Nadine and Maddie fell behind. They stopped by what he assumed was Dani's pitiful-looking car then circled it, cupping their hands and peering into the windows.

"Girls."

They jumped back from the car then scrambled over to his side.

Hiding a smile, he pointed at a large structure adjoining the back of the lodge. "That's the banquet hall. There's enough room for a hundred people or so but we don't use it very often because…" He shrugged, glancing over his shoulders at the empty fields and walkways. "I don't have as many guests as I'd like right now. But if things turn around like I hope, we'll be using it pretty regular." He shook his head. "I'd offer you a waitress or receptionist position but we don't need extra help in those areas."

"I didn't apply for a waitress or receptionist position." A hint of ice cooled the warm depths of her eyes and hardened her soft tone. "I'm here to work the grounds."

Nodding, he rolled his shoulders then motioned toward the graveled path behind them. "Then let's get moving."

The rocks crunched under his boots and the familiar sounds of the valley rushed in, filling his veins with excitement and lifting his chest with pride. He studied her face and noted the appreciative gleam in her expression.

"This land's been in my family for generations." He swept an arm toward the green fields, wooded landscape and hazy mountains in the distance. "We've got over thirty-six acres, twenty cabins and forty horses. There are hiking and horseback-riding trails. My lead hands are Tim Barnes and Cal McCoy. Tim leads two hiking groups each day and Cal heads up the riding excursions. They're working on the fence at the entrance. I assume you met them on the way in?" She nodded jerkily and he stopped, gesturing toward the log building in front of them. "There's the bunkhouse."

Dani adjusted her grip on her bag, her slim fingers tightening around it as she studied the bunkhouse.

"That's where the ranch hands stay," Nadine said, grabbing at Dani's bag. "You want me to help you put your stuff up?"

"No, Nadine." Mac gently brushed her hands aside. "I don't think Ms. Dani would like it there." He raised an eyebrow and smiled. "Unless, of course, you'd prefer to stay in the bunkhouse with the men? I think there's an empty bunk below Cal's."

Her cheeks reddened. "No, thank you." She bit her lip. "Is there another option?"

His smile widened. "Yep. That is, if I decide to hire you. I haven't said one way or the other yet."

Her pretty blush deepened and Mac moved further up the winding path through a cluster of cedar trees to a cabin. The weathered wood and sun-bleached porch rails were littered with leaves.

He grimaced. "Looks worse than it is. I haven't had time to restore the exterior but I cleaned up inside last week." The porch steps creaked as he ascended them. "There's one bedroom, one bathroom and a small kitchen and den."

"I'm not picky." The sweet sound of her voice sent thrills up his spine. "But won't you need this for guests?"

He glanced over his shoulder. She stood on the second step, Nadine and Maddie close at her side, and stared up at him.

His jaw clenched. "Not until the lodge fills ups. And that hasn't happened, yet." He opened the door then crossed the threshold. "Come on in."

A flurry of movement from the other side of the room caught his eye. Two legs and a muddy pair of boots darted behind the worn couch in the center of the den. Streaks of mud and clumps of dirt dulled the shine he'd spent hours buffing into the ancient hardwood floor just days ago.

Irritation sparked in his gut. "Jaxon." He bit his tongue, trying to soften the hard edge of his tone. "Get your tail out here."

Grubby fingers gripped the back of the couch then brown hair and green eyes rose above them.

"What are you doing in here? I asked you to stay in the game room with your sisters." Mac stiffened, Dani's light tread approaching behind him. He motioned toward the eyes peeping over the couch. "Dani, this is my son, Jaxon."

Jaxon stood then rounded the couch, his arms behind his back and his ten-year-old frame stiff. He studied Dani, the shaggy ends of his brown hair falling forward, brushing his eyebrows. The strands were the same shade as his mother's.

A stabbing pain shot thorough Mac. He hunched his shoulders and motioned toward Jaxon's obscured arms. "What have you got there?"

Jaxon scowled. "You said you were gonna take the day off and play baseball with me. I'm tired of babysitting."

Mac sighed. So was Ann. But he couldn't afford to hire a babysitter on a permanent basis. Or take a day off work like he'd planned. Not if he expected to hold on to this place. "I just asked you to stay put for an hour—not babysit."

"We ain't babies," Nadine said.

"Yeah," Maddie added.

"Aw, hush up." Jaxon's eyes flashed. "No one asked you two."

"That's enough. All of you." Mac dragged a hand over the back of his neck, the weight of Dani's stare heating his face. "It took me hours to clean this place up, Jaxon. You're going to spend the afternoon scrubbing this floor. Now, show me what you've got behind your back because I swear, if you've gotten into Tim's tools again—"

"I ain't got any tools." Jaxon stalked over and thrust a bundle against Mac's gut. "You promised you were gonna play ball with me."

Mac looked down, catching the baseball glove before it fell. Deep croaks, muffled by the mitt, vibrated the material against his hand. He unfolded it and a muddy bullfrog sprang from the center then plopped onto the floor.

Maddie squealed and hid her face against the back of his thigh. "Ew."

"Cool." Nadine chased it through the door and down the front steps.

Something else was lodged in the top portion of the mitt. Mac thumbed smudges of mud away from the paper-thin item, revealing a familiar smile. His throat thickened as he studied the well-worn photo of his late wife. The shape of Nicole's eyes and nose were exact replicas of Jaxon's.

"You promised."

Mac blinked hard and glanced up.

Jaxon glared at him but his chin trembled and his eyes glistened.

Gut churning, Mac said gently, "I'm sorry, Jaxon. I'll make it up to you. I promise—"

"Yeah, right." Jaxon snatched the glove back, shoved past him and stomped out of the cabin.

"Why's he so mean all the time?" Maddie asked, poking her head around his thigh and frowning up at him.

Mac forced a smile and tugged the pink ribbon brushing her cheek. "He's not mean, baby. He just…" *Misses his mother.* Mac swallowed hard. God help him, so did he. "He just needs his space once in a while. That's all." He motioned toward the door. "Why don't you play outside with your sister for a few minutes while I talk to Ms. Dani?"

"Yes, sir." Maddie brushed a speck of dirt off her sundress then skipped outside.

"Don't wander off, all right?" Mac called after her. "Stay near the cabin."

He relaxed slightly at her affirmative response then thrust his fists in his jeans pockets and avoided Dani's eyes. "Sorry about that."

She was silent for a moment then her soft voice drifted in, soothing the tight knot in his neck. "It's okay." Her footsteps drew closer. "I don't mean to pry but…is your wife here?"

"Nicole passed away four years ago. The girls were too young to remember her but Jaxon does."

Mac cringed at the gruff sound of his voice. He walked to the door and peered out against the glare of the midmorning sun. Nadine chased the bullfrog across the grass while Maddie picked wildflowers nearby. Jaxon was nowhere to be found. As usual.

Mac closed his eyes, his limbs heavy.

"I'm sorry to hear that," Dani whispered.

"They're normally not underfoot," he said. "But it's July and school's out so they wander around from time to time. Just don't mind them and go about your business as usual."

"Does that mean I have the job?" Dani's voice was hesitant. "Because if so, I think I should tell you now that…that I'm really…"

He opened his eyes and faced her. She stared at the muddy streaks marring the floor and her fingers picked at the hem of her T-shirt. Her soft curves and gentle tone made him yearn to cross the room to her side, ask her to wrap those slender arms around him and hug him close. Have someone hold *him* for a change.

She met his eyes and hitched the bag strap higher on her shoulder. "I'm actually here to—"

The strap snapped and her bulky bag slammed to the floor, clothing spilling from the gaping hole left behind. An unladylike word burst from her lips.

Blushing, she knelt beside the bag, gathering up lacy bras and ragged T-shirts then shoving them back inside. "Sorry." She puffed a wisp of hair out of her face. "That was rude."

A rusty chuckle stirred in Mac's chest. Smothering it, he grinned and tried his best to keep his gaze from straying to her tempting cleavage. "You really do need this job, don't you?"

Her hands stilled. "Honestly?" She looked up, eyes lingering on his smile. "I really do need to be here. And woman or not, I know I can help you." Her slim throat moved on a hard swallow. "If you give me a chance to prove it, I promise you won't regret it."

Mac's smile slipped at the shift in her tone. A strange coldness trickled into his gut and pricked at his skin.

"Trial basis." He forced the words past stiff lips. "It'll only take a day or two for me to see if you can hack it."

Chapter Two

Dani was going to hell—straight down a hole she'd dug herself. And she was tempted to drag lead hand, Cal McCoy, with her.

"Now this here is what we call an ax." Cal's mouth—still chewing on that filthy straw of hay from earlier—delivered each syllable with slow, exaggerated movements. He eased the tool closer to her face, pointed a blunt finger at the sharp end and raised his brows. "And this here is the blade."

Dani narrowed her eyes on the scruffy cowboy in front of her, a spark of anger overtaking the guilt that had lodged in her gut one hour earlier during her conversation with Mac. Only ten minutes in Cal's presence and she was ready to flip her wig. How in the world was she going to hold on to her temper long enough to secure this job?

"And this here..." Cal grabbed a log from the ground, balanced it in his palm then hefted it in front of his chest. "This here is what we call wood."

"Butthead."

Choking back a laugh at the muttered insult, Dani glanced over her shoulder.

Jaxon stood several feet away, leaning against a

fence and tossing a baseball into the glove on his hand. Just as he had for the past ten minutes as Cal led her through her first assigned task on the ranch.

"What was that, boy?" Cal frowned at Jaxon, the hay dangling precariously from the corner of his chapped lips.

Jaxon looked away and thrust the baseball harder into his glove. "Nothing. Sorry, sir."

"You got fire, kid," Cal said, laughing. "I'll give you that. Ain't you supposed to be babysitting? Your dad's havin' a time keeping up with those sisters of yours and getting the hikers started."

Jaxon stared down at his glove and didn't answer.

Dani leaned to the side and peered over Cal's shoulder. A small group of guests was gathered at the edge of a nearby field, packing backpacks and listening to Mac's instructions for the impending hike.

Mac gestured toward Tim, who stepped forward and took over speaking to the group, then knelt beside his daughters. He tugged something from his back pocket, pulled one twin close and started brushing her hair.

Judging from the girl's muddy jeans and unhappy expression, Dani guessed it was Nadine. She craned her neck for a clearer view and smiled, the sight of Mac's big hands moving gently over the girl's long hair stirring warm flutters in her belly and an ache in her chest.

When she'd concocted this plan to gain access to Mac, she'd expected to meet a ruthless man holding out for top dollar in a deal. Not a grieving father who loved his children and was clearly in over his head.

And she'd lied to him.

That ache in her chest tightened and a bead of sweat trickled across her temple. It didn't matter if she'd never intentionally deceived someone before. She'd done it today.

"…heard a word I just said?"

Dani snapped back to attention, her gaze jerking from Mac to Cal's disgruntled face. "What?"

Cal rolled his eyes. "Whatever you missed, girlie, I ain't got time to explain it again. And if you were a man, I wouldn't have to explain it at all." He tossed the ax in the dirt at her feet then ambled off, saying over his shoulder, "Just split those piles of wood and stack them. You got one hour."

Dani frowned. Jaxon was right. *Butthead* fit the bill perfectly.

She stared at the high pile of thick logs and shook her head. Female pride or not, if she had any sense, she'd grab her tattered bag, hop in that pathetic car and burn rubber back to New York.

Her shoulders sagged. But that would mean standing in the boardroom and facing a roomful of male executives—including her father. And what would she say? *Sorry, Dad. I know I promised to make this deal but…*

But what? She'd failed to deliver yet again? Prove that he'd been right all along and she wasn't equipped to run the company? That she was just another spoiled, rich girl who couldn't pull her own weight?

"Do you know what you're doing?"

Dani looked over her shoulder. Jaxon straddled the top rung of the fence and stared intently at her. His green eyes held no mockery or disdain. Just a concerned, empathetic light. And the kind note in his small voice made her think he knew much more than foolish men like Cal gave him credit for.

"No," she said. "I don't."

Jaxon glanced down and shrugged. "I could help you. I mean…if you wanted me to, I could."

She smiled, her heart melting for this boy who'd lost so much, and whispered, "That'd be great. Thank you."

He looked up, revealing a crooked grin.

Dani's breath caught. The tilt of his mouth was so similar to his father's brief smile earlier. The one that had lifted the sagging fatigue from Mac's muscular frame and the heavy shadows from his handsome face. The one that had made it too difficult to come clean entirely and risk adding to the painful load he carried.

"Okay." Jaxon straightened on the fence rung and gestured toward the stacks of wood. "First, you gotta pick out the best logs. My dad says the seasoned ones with the cracks in 'em are the easiest to break."

Dani nodded then sifted through several logs before hefting one out of the pile and tilting it toward Jaxon. She drifted a finger along a deep crack in the wood. "Like this?"

"Yeah." He pointed at a large stump on the ground. "Now, put it on that and hit it right on the split."

She set the log on the stump, steadied it then grabbed the ax. "All right." Taking a deep breath, she lifted the ax and started to swing. "Here we go."

"Wait!"

Dani jumped and her hands slipped on the ax handle. The tool plunged to the ground, slicing into the dirt and lodging dangerously close to the toe of her sneaker.

"Sorry." Jaxon winced. "But if you stand like that, you're gonna chop your foot off."

She raised an eyebrow, a humorless laugh bursting from her lips. "Sure looks that way."

Jaxon hopped off the fence, tossed his baseball glove on the grass and walked over. "You gotta stand wide and bend your knees." He tapped her insteps with his boot until her stance met his approval then squatted slightly and held his hands up as though gripping the ax. "Like this, see? One hand high and one hand low."

Dani grinned, grabbed the ax and mimicked his posture. "This way?"

"Yep." Jaxon smiled and tossed his brown hair out of his eyes. "Dad splits two piles every day and saves 'em up for the cabins during winter. He lets me help sometimes. He told me it ain't about strength. It's about finesse."

Those warm flutters returned to her belly. She glanced across the field. Mac stood still, eyes fixed firmly on her and Jaxon, as his daughters chased each other by his side.

"You need gloves, you know?" Jaxon added. "And glasses. At least, that's what my dad says. He doesn't let me practice without 'em. Says it's better to be safe than sorry. You could ask him." Jaxon's voice hardened. "But he's probably too busy to get 'em for you."

Mac lifted a hand to his forehead and squinted against the sun, his scrutiny more intense.

Cheeks heating, Dani tore her gaze away. "I'll be careful." She adjusted her grip on the ax and tipped her chin toward the fence. "Jaxon, could you please watch from over there? I'd feel better if you were out of the danger zone."

He nodded, darted off then ducked between the fence rungs.

She eyed the thick log standing on the wide stump, steadied her stance and swung. The blade stabbed into the surface of the wood and stuck, the impact rever-berating down her arms.

"Take it out and hit it again." Jaxon climbed on to the fence.

Dani smiled, pried the ax from the log then struck it harder. The blade landed perfectly, a heavy thud echoing across the valley, but the log didn't split.

Her back and shoulders were another matter. Every muscle in her upper body stretched with strain, screaming that she'd pay for this later.

Jaxon smacked the fence rung with his palms. "You got perfect aim. Better than Mr. Cal."

Dani laughed, the excitement on his face easing the painful throb in her arms. "Really? You're not just trying to make me feel better, are you?"

"Heck no. You're a better shot than him any day." He grinned and bounced on the fence rung. "Flip it over and do it again."

She did. Two more swift strokes of the ax and a satisfying crack rang out as the wood split, toppling off the stump and onto the ground in even halves.

Dani tipped her head back, heaved out a satisfied breath and closed her eyes. The sun's heat seeped into her skin, her muscles tightening deliciously and a sweet satisfaction vibrating within her.

Take that, suits. She laughed. This was something those stuffy executives could never experience behind an office desk or in a corporate boardroom.

"You're good." Jaxon hopped off the fence, scooped up his baseball glove and tugged it on. "Better than good." He crossed to her side, pounding a fist in the mitt. "You play baseball? 'Cuz I bet you'd be killer at bat."

"Yeah. I like baseball." She bent, grabbed another log and balanced it on the stump. "I watch the Mets on TV quite a bit but it's been years since I've played."

"The Mets?" His brow furrowed. "You from New York?"

Dani froze, the log's bark rough against her palm. She glanced up and the innocent curiosity on the boy's face intensified the churn in her stomach. "Yes."

He mulled this over for a moment then asked, "How'd you end up here?"

She swallowed the thick lump in her throat. "It's complicated." *And shameful.* Which made her a straight-up awful person. She ducked her head and resumed her chopping stance. "I should get back to work. And you should probably check in with your dad. Thanks for the help."

Jaxon kicked the ground and spun away. "Whatever."

The hurt note in his tone sent a fresh wave of guilt through her. "Hey." She waited until he stopped, back planted to her. "There's no way I could've done this without your help. And I really do enjoy your company. I just need to finish this, okay?"

He looked over his shoulder, voice hesitant. "So can I stay and watch? I promise I won't get in the way."

What was it Mac had said? *Just don't mind them and go about your business as usual.*

Dani's eyes returned to Mac. He'd rejoined the group of guests and carried on a conversation with one of them, his daughters at his side, but he kept shooting looks at her.

She faced Jaxon and studied the hopeful light in his expression. It was so familiar. That vulnerable look of wanting to be given admittance. Wanting to belong and not be brushed aside. It was a feeling she knew all too well.

"Of course," she said. "I'd like that."

Smiling, he hustled to the fence and climbed up again, settling on the top rung.

Dani faced the log, tightened her grip on the ax handle then swung. An hour passed with rhythmic thuds of the ax. Sharp cracks of wood and Jaxon's baseball pounding into his glove reverberated across the grounds. Sweat streamed down her face and back, her soaked shirt clinging to her skin with each swing.

She struck the wood harder and tried not to think about Jaxon, his sisters or their handsome dad. Instead, she paused between each stroke of the ax and took mental notes of the ranch's layout.

Three paddocks with worn fences were stationed near a large stable. The stable looked sound and efficient but the outside walls were weathered and unattractive.

A fat drop of sweat stung her eye and she flinched, blinking it away to view the structure more clearly. Hmm. Some red paint, a bit of white trim and several strategically placed azaleas and it'd be much more appealing to the eye. It would also induce that good old-fashioned nostalgic feel a lot of people sought when choosing a place to stay in the Smokies.

Body aching, she paused, grabbed the split halves of wood then stacked them in a slowly growing pile. The grounds were in much the same state as the secluded cabin where she'd stowed her bag. So much potential but too much neglect.

"Want me to take over for a while?"

Dani dragged the back of her hand across her sweat-slickened forehead then smiled at Jaxon. "No, thanks."

"But you look tired." He frowned, peering over her shoulder. "And they're laughing at you."

She glanced around. The group of guests had left for their hike with Tim, and the girls were no longer in the field playing. But Cal and several other hands stood by the fence of a neighboring paddock, sipping from water bottles and grinning as they leered in her direction.

"It's okay." Dani hefted the ax into her hands, renewed her grip and smiled. "Let them laugh. I'm used to it."

Jaxon smiled back but whispered, "You're all red, though. And you really do look tired."

"He has a point."

Big palms settled on the wood handle between her smaller ones and Mac, solemn-faced, stared down at her.

"The stalls need mucking," Mac said, eyeing her and tugging on the ax. "You can do that instead."

She tugged back. "But I'm getting it done and there's a lot more to split."

"Yeah, and at the rate you're going, it'll take you a week to finish." His expression softened. "You're getting it done. Just not fast enough." He pulled the ax from her grip. "I've got time to finish this stack now and I'll do the second one in the morning."

"But—"

"The shovel and wheelbarrow are in the stable store room. Remove the waste, add clean shavings then dump the load out back." He grabbed a log and steadied it on the stump. "When you finish, see Cal and he'll tell you what to do next."

He positioned his muscular bulk in front of the stump, his hard jean-clad hip brushing against her soft middle.

Her heart tripped in her chest and she stepped back, thighs trembling from her earlier exertions. Gritting her teeth, she forced out, "I can finish this."

"I'm sure you can," Mac said, lifting the ax. "But I'd prefer it if you'd clean the stalls."

A fresh round of male laughter cracked the silence of the fields.

"Break's over," Mac shouted. He stepped in front of her and faced the hands. "Get back to work."

They stopped laughing and dispersed.

Dani froze, staring at Mac's broad back. Things were no different here than they were in New York. Here, she was brushed aside just as carelessly as in the Vaughn boardroom. Mac and these men didn't see her. They saw only what they wanted to see—a weak woman.

Face burning, Dani spun on her heels and started toward the stable. Jaxon scowled at his father then hopped off the fence as she passed.

"Jaxon," Mac called. "Go inside with your sisters."

Footsteps drew closer at Dani's back. "I'm gonna help Ms. Dani."

"I said, go inside."

The footsteps quickened and Jaxon sprang past her then ran into the stable.

Dani stopped. Mac stared at the entrance of the stable where Jaxon had entered and the look of angry helplessness on his face returned the ache to her chest, forcing her pride to lower its ugly head.

Catching her eyes on him, he jerked back to the wood in front of him, swung the ax and split the wood in one stroke. She watched for a minute then joined Jaxon in the stable. Jaxon no longer smiled or asked questions as she worked. He just shoveled silently by her side.

Dani wheeled the first cart of waste out back, dumped it and stared at the foggy mountainside. The guilty pang of having lied returned. Her presence at Elk Valley exacerbated whatever rift existed between Mac and his son. And her conscience, overruling her pride, wouldn't allow her to carry on with this charade.

No matter how much Cal laughed…or how many times Mac dismissed her.

For Jaxon's sake, she'd leave first thing in the morning. But before she crawled into the cabin's rickety bed tonight, she'd prove Mac wrong. That second pile of wood would be split and stacked before the sun rose. Even if it killed her.

PREDICTABILITY ENSURED SECURITY. Risk invited chaos. Mac firmly believed both.

"But why?" Nadine flopped back against her pillow, crossed her arms over the pink blanket he'd tugged over her and frowned. "Why can't we go hiking with the group tomorrow? Ms. Dani said a girl can do anything she sets her mind to."

Ms. Dani, again. Mac sighed and sat on the edge of the bed in the twins' bedroom. After he and the kids had retired to the family floor of the lodge for the night, Nadine and Jaxon had talked about Dani nonstop through dinner. It was unsettling how quickly they'd attached to her.

"Ms. Dani is right. But she's also an adult who can take care of herself. You and Maddie, however, are too young to take off by yourself and Mr. Tim can't lead the group and supervise the two of you. Besides, a storm is supposed to roll in midafternoon and I don't want you or your sister stranded on a mountainside when it tears through. And because…"

Because I have hours of work tomorrow—including splitting an extra stack of wood and clearing the lower hayfield. And because Tim might turn his back for a second and you'll run off. Get lost. Hurt. Or worse.

Mac frowned and tapped her small chin with a knuckle. "I'd rather you and Maddie stay here where I can keep an eye on you." Or at least try to. He grinned. "I promise when the weather's right and things settle down, I'll take you, Maddie and Jaxon hiking myself. We'll climb and—"

"Fish?" Nadine asked.

"Yes. And have a campfire and—"

"Roast marshmallows?" Maddie piped from the twin bed across the room, grinning. "I like the marshmallow part better than the fishing part."

Mac laughed then stood. "First, we'll go fishing." He bent, kissed Nadine's forehead then crossed the room and kissed Maddie's. "Then, we'll roast as many marshmallows as that little belly of yours can hold."

"Did Mama like roasting marshmallows?" Maddie leaned up on her elbows, brushed the ever-present pink bow from her eyes and blinked up at him. "Is that why I like them so much?"

Mac's breath caught in his throat, making it difficult to speak. Roasting marshmallows was one of the few things Nicole had liked about hiking and camping. She'd never been a fan of the outdoors. Not even when they were teens. But she'd loved snuggling by the campfire and sharing marshmallows with him. *That part's the sweetest*, she'd always said.

"Yeah," he whispered. "She did. That was always her favorite part."

Mac cleared his throat and walked to the door.

"Dad?"

His hand stilled on the doorknob. Nadine smiled gently at him, a hint of sadness in her eyes. As though she knew...

"It's okay if we don't go hiking tomorrow." She shrugged. "We'll find something else to do."

Mac's smile returned. "I'm sure you will. But please check with me before you do it and no running off without telling anyone. Now, go to sleep."

He made his way through the family wing of the lodge to the next bedroom then hesitated, fist lifted, at the closed door. Nadine and Maddie might not be stress-free but at least they were easy to talk to. Jaxon, not so much.

"Jaxon?" He knocked then cracked the door open. "You ready for bed?"

A bed creaked and sheets rustled. "Yeah."

Mac entered, stooping to pick up a pair of muddy jeans, several baseball cards and a glove then toss each in its proper place. "Thanks for cleaning the cabin floor today. You did a good job."

Jaxon sat up in the bed, a small smile appearing.

Mac's throat thickened. Lord, it'd been so long since he'd seen Jaxon smile, he'd forgotten how much it eased his mind and brightened the day. It'd hit him hard earlier this afternoon when he'd watched Jaxon share a laugh with Dani. That was the first time Jaxon had laughed in ages.

"Think you could clean up just as well in here tomorrow?" he asked, glancing around.

The lamp's low glow highlighted little-boy clutter from one corner of the room to the other. Darts, baseballs, rumpled papers and toy guns littered the nightstand, dresser and chest of drawers. And dirty clothes, comic books and socks were strewn across the carpet.

"It'd be a tough job. But…" Mac narrowed his eyes and rubbed his chin. "I think a hardworking man like you can handle it."

Jaxon's smile widened. "Yeah. I can do it." He cocked an eyebrow. "Does that mean you're gonna increase my allowance?"

"Don't push it." Mac grinned, ruffled his hair then reached for the lamp switch.

Jaxon grabbed his wrist and peered up at him. "Ms. Dani did a good job today, too. Didn't she?"

Mac hesitated, studying the hopeful gleam in Jaxon's eyes. "I suppose she did."

"Then why'd you make her clean the stalls instead of chopping the wood?"

"Well, she was obviously worn out. And sunburned. And…"

Sweaty. So sweaty that her clothes had stuck to her. With the sun at her back, her every swing of the ax drew more male attention to her enticing curves. Almost every hand he employed had lined the fence to gawk, crack lewd jokes and mock her. And, even though she'd seemed oblivious to it, he'd been damned if he'd allow it to continue.

"She's got good aim, you know?" Jaxon said, leaning forward. "Better than Mr. Cal. And she likes baseball, too. Said she watches the Mets. I told her she'd be killer at bat. Did you know she's from New York?"

Mac frowned as Jaxon paused to catch his breath. "New York?" She hadn't listed any prior residences or work experience in New York on her application. "What makes you think that?"

"She told me so." His face lit up. "I bet she'd play ball with me. She said she liked having me around and could use my help. So can I help her again tomorrow? You are gonna hire her, aren't you?"

"Slow down, Jaxon." Mac placed his hands on his shoulders and eased him back against the pillows. "We just met her and I can't say for sure if I'll be able to hire her or not. Besides, I think you're spending too much time with her as it is."

All afternoon, in fact. Jaxon had trailed after Dani the entire day, only returning to the lodge when she'd knocked off for the night and joined the other hands in the commons for supper. Mac stiffened. His intense attraction to Dani unnerved him enough on its own. But the contradictions surrounding her and her dodgy mannerisms caused him even more concern. Especially when it came to Jaxon and Nadine who were both clearly taken with her.

"Why? I ain't bothering her. I'm helping."

"I know but I'm telling you to ease up." Mac braced his hands on the mattress and leaned close. "And I expect you to obey me when I ask you to do something.

As in earlier this afternoon, when I asked you to come inside with your sisters and you disobeyed me instead."

The last remnants of Jaxon's smile vanished. His face flushed and he burrowed deeper into the bed, pulling the sheet up to his chin. "I'm sorry. I just wanted to hang out with her." He bit his lip. "She listens to me and...likes having me around."

Unlike you. Mac flinched, the unspoken phrase darkening Jaxon's gaze and thickening the air between them.

"*I* like having you around." Mac cupped a hand around Jaxon's head. "And I promise you—" Jaxon moved to speak and Mac firmed his features. "I *promise* that when things slow up, we'll spend more time together."

Jaxon stared up at him, eyes doubtful. "When?"

"When I get this place back in order. But for now, I need you to be patient and do as I say."

Jaxon nodded reluctantly then rolled over, his back and shoulders stiff.

Mac kissed the top of his head. "Good night, Jaxon."

He received no response. As expected.

Mac turned the lamp off and left, striding swiftly down the winding staircase to the front porch. He leaned on the porch rail, the screen door slamming shut behind him, and sucked in a ragged breath.

Damn. He'd screwed up. Again. He hated dictating orders to Jaxon. Arguing with him. Offering weak platitudes in place of actually spending quality time with his son. He was a weak, pathetic excuse for a father and Nicole would be disappointed in him.

Head pounding, he rubbed his forehead and stared at the starlit sky above him. But what was he supposed to do? Call it quits? Sell the ranch, uproot his kids and hope he had better luck elsewhere?

He'd barely survived losing Nicole to cancer. Losing his family's land—the only tangible memory he had left of his deceased parents—might just finish him off.

The incessant pounding grew stronger and he stilled, realizing the heavy thumps weren't just in his head. They echoed across the grounds, too. He shoved off the porch rail and followed the sound, his steps halting beside the stable.

Dani stood in front of the chopping stump, the waning moon overhead and a camping lantern at her feet casting competing glows of white and yellow light against her curvy figure. She swung an ax and split a log. Shifting the ax to one hand, she grabbed one half of the split log and tossed it onto a freshly cut pile of wood, her long ponytail swinging across her upper back.

"Working late, huh?"

She jumped and spun around, hand pressing to her chest. Her eyes narrowed as they peered into the darkness surrounding him. "Good grief, you scared me."

He stepped into the pool of light, smiling gently. "Sorry. I didn't mean to. I heard the noise from the lodge and thought I'd check it out."

She nodded then turned away and grabbed the second half of the split log.

"You don't have to do this, you know?" Mac gestured toward the ax at her side. "I told you I'd take care of it in the morning."

"After you let me down easy?" She shrugged and tossed the log onto the pile. "Figured I'd earn my stay tonight before I move on tomorrow." Pausing, she studied the ax handle then glanced at him. "Thank you for offering me a chance here but I don't think this is going to work out for either one of us."

He blinked, chin lifting as he examined her face. "What makes you say that?"

Her head tilted and a humorless smile spread slowly across her face. "Well, let's see. I wasn't what you were expecting. You don't think I can pull my weight." She ticked each concern off on her fingertips. "You banished me to the stable to scoop poop, as Nadine puts it, because I wasn't passing muster with the ax—"

"Now, hold up." He held up a hand. "That's not true. The fact of the matter was half my hands had lined up to ogle you while you worked and I was—"

"Protecting the weak, trouble-stirring girl?" Her eyebrows rose. "Telling me what I could and couldn't do for my own good?"

"No." He clenched his teeth, a streak of anger burning his gut. "I was trying to be a gentleman."

She stared, shoulders dropping and head lowering. "I appreciate that," she whispered. "But I've had enough of men telling me what I can and can't do. It'd just be really nice to have a choice for a change."

The resigned look on her face tempered his frustration. "Not all men are the same. I didn't mean to offend you."

She smiled. A real one that sent a rush of pleasure through his veins. "Not all women are the same. And I'm sorry I took offense."

Mac shoved his hands in his pockets as she retrieved another log and balanced it on the stump. "So where you movin' on to? Back to New York?"

Dani sprang upright and faced him, expression guarded.

He examined her more closely, trepidation creeping up his spine. "Jaxon said you told him that's where you're from."

Her features relaxed and she nodded. "Yes. That's where I'm headed."

"What do you do there?" He gestured toward the stack of firewood. "I don't get the impression that you've been doing this type of work for very long."

Her stance stiffened. "I'm in…sales."

"What kind of sales?"

"The boring kind." She sighed. "The kind that keeps you holed up in an office staring at walls all day."

"So you came here for a change of scenery?"

"I suppose you could say that." She hesitated, voice softening. "I definitely needed a change and it is beautiful here." She hefted the ax into her hands, shooting glances at him. "I enjoyed spending time with Jaxon today. He's a wonderful child."

Mac smiled. "That he is."

"He admires you a lot and talks about you often," she said. "He told me about how you taught him to split wood and how important his safety is to you."

His face heated and he looked away. "Yeah, well, everyone has to pitch in around here to keep things running."

"He misses you."

Mac's eyes jerked back to hers, the pointed look filling the blue depths conjuring deep-seated guilt. "Putting the shoe on the other foot now, huh?" he asked. "Giving the man pointers on parenting? Going to tell me what a bad father I am?"

"No." She looked genuinely appalled. "God, no. If anything, I'd say the opposite. I may have only been here a day but it's obvious how much you love Jaxon. And Nadine and Maddie."

He stared down at his boots, the heat in his cheeks scorching down his neck. Her words lingered in his head then eased into his chest, delivering a sense of comfort that he wanted to hold on to.

"I don't have children and I have no clue what it's like being a single parent." Her scuffed sneakers appeared in his line of vision and the fresh scent of grass and sun-seasoned wood drifted in. "But I know what it's like to want to be seen. Noticed. My father is a hard worker like you and when I was young, he'd always say we'd spend time together. Tomorrow or the next day. But time got away from him and it just never happened. Our relationship hasn't been the same since." Her tone softened. "That's all Jaxon wants. To be seen. Noticed."

He raised his head, finding her closer than he'd expected. The once-creamy skin of her cheeks and forehead was sunburned a cherry red and freckles were scattered across the bridge of her nose, giving her an earthy, attractive air. Her wide eyes blinked up at him, patient and kind, then focused on his mouth and darkened.

She stepped back and shook her head. "Anyway, it's my turn to apologize. It's none of my business and I didn't mean to offend you. I like Jaxon and just thought I'd give you my two cents before I left."

She moved farther away and resumed splitting wood, her movements slow and unsteady.

Mac hesitated then went into the stable and fumbled through a couple shelves in the storage room until he found a pair of small gloves. He returned to Dani and held them out.

"Here. You'll wake up with more blisters than you can count if you don't put these on. They'll be too big but will help at least. And breakfast is at six if you'd like to have a decent meal before you leave tomorrow."

She paused between swings, breathing heavily, and took the gloves. "Thank you."

"You're welcome."

He hovered, waiting as she tugged on the gloves then returned to the task at hand. He headed back to the lodge, walking carefully along the moonlit stone path, and listened as the strokes of the ax echoed across the fields.

There was no need to mull over whether or not to hire Dani. She'd decided to leave on her own accord. That thought alone should ease his worries. She'd been a risky hire from the start and she was still far too guarded for his peace of mind. But in just one day, she'd made Jaxon smile more than he'd managed to in months.

So...what if he asked her to stay?

His steps slowed. With a new hand, he'd be freed from chores more often and would actually be able to follow through with some of his promises to Jaxon. But he'd have to invest a great deal of time in training her for the job first. And judging from today, he'd bet it wouldn't be a smooth transition with the rest of the hands.

Mac stopped and looked back. Either way, Dani had a point. If he didn't try something different soon, he could lose a lot more than his land. He could lose the respect of his son.

Chapter Three

This was either the best decision Mac had ever made or the worst. At the moment, he couldn't tell for sure which one it'd turn out to be.

"Want me to climb through the window?"

Mac stopped knocking on the door of Dani's cabin and glanced down at Jaxon. "No. Absolutely not."

But he had to do something. He was beginning to worry.

After a night of tossing and turning, he'd gotten out of bed this morning with the express purpose of offering Dani the job and asking her to stay. But she hadn't shown up for breakfast, much to Jaxon and Nadine's disappointment, and no one had seen her all morning. Eight in the morning elsewhere might be considered early, but at Elk Valley Ranch it was the equivalent of noon.

She hadn't left yet. Her tattered car still sat in the back parking lot where she'd parked it yesterday morning before starting work. But she hadn't answered the door, either. Even though he'd been banging on it and calling out to her for the past five minutes.

"I bet a bear got in there." Nadine lifted to the toes

of her unlaced shoes and peeked in the window. "He probably ate her."

Maddie, standing next to her, gasped. "Daddy! Did he really?"

Jaxon rolled his eyes and scoffed.

"No, Maddie." Mac rubbed his temples. "A bear did not eat Ms. Dani."

"How do you know?" Nadine pressed her nose to the glass, her expression at the thought of a bear invading the cabin much too giddy for Mac's liking. "Can you see her? Cuz I don't see nothing."

"Nadine, stop it. You're scaring your sister." Mac tugged her back to his side and tried once more. "Dani? You all right in there?"

No answer.

Mac hesitated, eyed the door then nudged Nadine toward Jaxon. "You three stay put here, okay?" He twisted the knob and cracked the door open. "I'll be back in a minute."

At Jaxon's nod, Mac slipped inside the cabin. Sunlight streamed in between the gaps in the curtains, glinting off a glass on the coffee table in the empty den and spilling across the floor of the kitchen. The door to the bedroom was open. He walked over to the threshold then paused. This room was empty as well, and the only sign of Dani's presence was a set of rumpled sheets on the unoccupied bed.

"Dani?"

A thump sounded on the other side of the closed bathroom door. "I'm in here. I've been answering you but I guess you couldn't hear me."

Mac relaxed at the muffled sound of her voice. "Are you okay?"

"Yeah. I just…" Her voice faded. "I took a shower and I've been trying to get dressed."

He ducked his head, shifting awkwardly from one boot to the other. "What do you mean, trying?"

"I mean…" The door creaked open and her hand, beet red and shaky, wrapped around the doorframe. "I've been trying. It took a while."

The rest of her slowly appeared. Her long legs, encased in jeans, moved stiffly and her arms—redder than her hands—were held out to each side, carefully keeping their distance from the rest of her body.

She looked up and flinched, the skin of her upper chest and face a fiery red so dark it was almost purple above her T-shirt. "I'm a little sore and I have a bit of a sunburn."

Mac smothered a laugh then cringed with sympathy. "A bit? Dani, you're redder than a cherry."

"But sweeter." She smiled. It disappeared abruptly as her cheeks stretched. "I knew I had one last night but I didn't know it was this bad."

"Yeah, well, chopping that second stack of wood doesn't look as though it did your muscles any favors, either." Mac held out his hand. "Here. Come sit for a minute and I'll rustle up some meds."

She stepped forward gingerly and took his hand. His thumb brushed across her overheated skin, the light connection stirring a sense of longing within him as he led her into the den.

"No bear." Nadine's voice was full of disappointment as she slumped over the back of the couch, her chin resting on the top cushion and arms dangling against the seat.

Jaxon and Maddie stood to the side with curious expressions.

Mac's lips twisted. "I thought I asked y'all to wait outside."

Nadine grinned. "We were worried."

"Yeah," Mac drawled. "I can see that." He motioned for her to move then assisted Dani as she lowered herself slowly onto the couch. "Jaxon, please take your sisters to the lodge and ask Ms. Ann for a bottle of aloe. Then bring it to me."

"You all right, Ms. Dani?" Jaxon asked.

Dani waved a hand in the air. "I'm fine. Just a sunburn and sore muscles is all."

Jaxon smiled and headed for the door, Nadine dashing after him. "We'll be back in a sec."

Their footsteps stampeded down the front steps then faded.

Mac glanced at Maddie who still stood motionless by the couch. "Maddie?"

The sweet smile she normally sported was gone, a frown having taken its place, as she stared. He followed her eyes and looked down, noticing his hand still cradled Dani's against her slim thigh.

He released it and straightened. "Maddie." She looked up at him. "Will you help your brother, please?"

She nodded then left, casting one more frown in Dani's direction.

Mac rubbed his hands over his jeans. "Sorry. I didn't mean for you to be invaded this morning."

Dani smiled then winced. "Ow." A soft laugh escaped her. "Have you noticed we do way too much apologizing to each other?"

Mac grinned. "Yeah."

Lord, she was cute. Even if her face was the shade of an overripe tomato. His smile fell. And he was a potential employer who had no business noticing how cute she was.

"That's got to stop." Avoiding her eyes, he grabbed the glass from the coffee table then walked into the kitchen. "There should be some ibuprofen in here. I stock travel packs of just about everything in the cabins for guests as a courtesy."

Dani made a soft sound of approval. "I noticed yesterday that you go above and beyond to make guests feel valued. You're a good manager."

He fished a packet of ibuprofen from a drawer then filled the glass with water. "I want people to enjoy their stay. Besides, providing extras is necessary to attract more business."

Mac returned to the living room and handed over the ibuprofen packet and water. "Get that in you. It'll help. Though you'll probably be even sorer tomorrow."

She smirked. "Good to know."

He waited as she took the pills and drank deeply from the cup then said, "I thought about what you said last night."

She paused, glancing at him over the rim of the glass.

"About time getting away." Mac sat beside her and propped his elbows on his knees. "Time is one thing I'm short on and having another hand on staff would help out a lot. Not just with the ranch. It'd give me more time with my kids, too." He met her eyes. "Especially, Jaxon."

She lowered the glass and looked away.

"I know you decided to leave today but I was hoping you'd think it over some more. The job's yours if you want it."

"I…" Her finger tapped against the cup, a wary look crossing her face. "I don't think that's a good idea."

"Why not? You need a job and I need help. You're the only applicant I've had for this job in months. I know the work is tough but—"

"It's not that."

"Then what is it? More pay?" He shook his head. "I'd give it to you if I had it, but things are tight—"

"No." Her voice was soft. So soft, he had to lean in to hear it. "The pay is fine. I'm just not what you're looking for."

He shifted uncomfortably. "I'll admit I was disappointed when I first met you yesterday." Her head rose, irritation flashing in her eyes. "But I felt differently last night. Watching you chop wood after hours…" He blew out a heavy breath. "Hell, it's been two years since an employee volunteered for overtime much less did it without my asking. I hadn't realized how apathetic the hands had become. Tim's about the only one who thinks I still have a chance of turning this place around and he's so concerned with not overstepping his boundaries that he never really tells me what's on his mind. At least you give it to me straight."

Dani folded her arms against her middle, eyes roving over his face. "Not always. We're practically strangers. You're only guessing at what I can offer you based on a late-night ax spree." She frowned. "I may not turn out to be the kind of person you think I am."

"That's even better." He smiled as confusion clouded her features. "You'll keep the other hands guessing. Maybe light a fire under them. We could use a little healthy competition around here." He nudged her knee with a knuckle. "Please just think about it. Unless, you've got something better waiting for you back in New York?"

She stilled then shoved awkwardly to her feet, brushing his hand away as he attempted to help her. "No. There's nothing better waiting for me in New York. But I'm not who you need." A pained expression crossed her face before she moved toward the bedroom. "I'm truly sorry, Mac."

His stomach sank and his limbs turned heavy. "I thought we were done apologizing."

Apparently, he'd have to count this idea of finding a new hand as another dead end. Another failed attempt at improving his chances of holding on to his land. As one more fruitless effort to secure more time with his children.

And oddly, the thought of Dani leaving spurred an additional churn in his gut. This attraction he had to her was unwelcome but at least it made him feel more like a man and less like an exhausted, inept dad.

Standing, he dragged a hand through his hair. "I respect your decision. I just wanted to be sure you knew the choice was yours."

She stopped and looked at him, surprise in her eyes.

Footsteps pounded up the steps then Jaxon ran inside. He drew to halt in front of Dani, a large bottle of aloe vera gel in his hand and a wide smile on his face. "I've got it!"

Thirty minutes later, Mac tossed Dani's bedraggled overnight bag into the passenger seat of her car and glanced up at the clouds encroaching on the sunny morning sky. He cringed, adding up the hours of work ahead and subtracting the minutes of daylight they'd already burned as Jaxon and Nadine pleaded with Dani by the driver's side door. There was next to no chance that he'd finish stacking the last of the hay before it rained this afternoon.

"Please stay, Ms. Dani," Jaxon said. "You did really good yesterday. Even Dad said so."

"And you're the only girl hand here." Nadine scowled. "When you leave, there'll be nothing but boys again."

"That's enough, kids." Mac leveled a stern look over the hood of the car. "Ms. Dani has made up her mind and there's a lot of work to do. It's time to wish her well and let her go on her way."

"Yeah. It's time for her to go," Maddie said, skipping over and slamming the passenger door shut. "Bye, Ms. Dani."

Mac frowned at the eagerness in Maddie's voice then whispered, "Don't be rude, Maddie."

She blushed. "Yes, sir."

Mac walked around the car to Dani's side and tugged his wallet out of his back pocket. "Before you leave, let me pay you what you're owed."

"Oh, no." Dani pushed his hands away and stepped back. "You don't owe me anything."

"You put in a full day of work yesterday plus overtime. That's worth more than two meals and one night's stay." He counted out an appropriate amount then lifted it toward her. "Here."

Strangely, her sunburned face flushed even redder. "I can't take that, Mac." She glanced quickly at the children then stepped closer and lowered her voice. "I only came because—"

"Calling it quits already, gal?"

Her expression froze at the sound of Cal's voice and her gaze drifted over his left shoulder.

Cal walked by, carrying a set of tools and grinning. "That's a smart decision. You look a little worse for wear and we're stacking hay today—those bales take muscle to move. If you stayed any longer, we'd find you keeled over in the barn by lunchtime."

"No you wouldn't." Jaxon shouldered his way between Mac and Dani. "She'd show you up any day."

Cal laughed. "Is that so?"

Mac frowned. "Knock it off, Cal."

"Aw, come on, Mac." Cal spread his hands. "I'm just foolin' around. Besides, you know it's true."

Dani scoffed. "Not necessarily."

Mac stilled, then ran his eyes over the ice in her blue eyes and tight set of her mouth. *Well, what do you know?* Dani didn't just have a temper, she had a healthy dose of pride, too. Even with a vicious sunburn and sore muscles. And it might be just the ticket to changing her mind and getting her to stay. Hell, if he failed, he had nothing to lose. As it was, he might actually have a shot at getting a full day's worth of work out of Cal, too.

"Care to wager a bet on that?" Mac asked.

Dani's attention jerked away from Cal and settled on him instead. "What?"

He cocked an eyebrow. "Well, you're not gonna let Cal tell you what you can and can't do, are you?"

The shot hit its mark. A muscle in her jaw clenched and she straightened.

"It'll be a simple competition," Mac said, grinning. "We'll split the hayloft in two. You'll take one side and

Cal will take the other. You'll each pick a partner and the first one to fill their side of the barn wins."

"What will she win, dad?" Jaxon asked, scooting closer to Dani's side and smiling.

"She?" Cal sputtered. "Y'all actually think this gal can stack bales faster than I can?"

"Well, we won't know until we see it," Mac said. "And the winner will name their own reward. Within reason, of course," he tacked on, eyeing Cal. "They'll also walk away having successfully proven their point."

"Well, hell," Cal said. "I'm in. This will be the easiest bonus I've ever earned."

Dani hesitated, her eyes moving from Mac to Cal then back again.

"Do it, Ms. Dani," Nadine whispered, tugging on her arm. "Show him up like Jaxon said."

"The winner names their own reward, right?" Dani asked. "I have your word on that?"

Mac met her eyes, his heart skipping at the secretive gleam in them. "You have my word."

Dani smiled. "All right. You have yourself a bet."

GRAB THE BALES off the hay elevator, stack them faster than Cal and an unimpeded hour-long sales pitch with Mac would be guaranteed.

Dani batted away a gnat then climbed up the barn ladder to the hayloft. That was all she needed—one hour. Once Mac heard her out, he'd understand she'd had good intentions coming here and after she delivered her best sales pitch he would see the benefits of selling his land. Or, at least, she hoped he would. Then, she'd be on her way back to New York with a clean conscience and deed in hand.

"Over here." A big hand cupped her elbow and steered her toward the open door of the hayloft. "Your gloves on good?"

Dani nodded and looked up, her determined focus fading beneath the sexy pull of Mac's green eyes. The thick waves of his blond hair ruffled as the wind surged across the field and gusted into the loft. He peered at the dark clouds building in the sky then frowned.

"These summer storms blow in fast. Time to get moving." Mac motioned toward the group of men standing below them by a tractor. "Hit it!"

An engine roared to life and the long, metal shaft propped at the loft's opening moved, the chains squeaking and clanking as they rotated.

"Jim—the guy by the trailer—will load the bales on the elevator and keep count." Mac pointed to the loft's dimly lit interior. "That side is yours. When the bales come off the elevator, you'll need to grab 'em, toss 'em, then stack 'em. Cal has chosen Tim as his partner."

"And who's my partner?"

"Me." Mac smiled. "Unless you prefer working with someone else?"

Something fluttered in her chest. She cleared her throat, a grin fighting its way to her lips. "No. I suppose you'll do."

He tilted his head back and laughed. The action coaxed her eyes to the attractive grooves lining his mouth and the charming dimple in his chin.

Oh, how he would do...

That fluttering sensation spread, stealing her breath. She mentally kicked herself. *Get it together. Forget the silly dimple and focus on why you're here.*

Heavy steps echoed against the wooden walls of

the loft as Cal stepped off the top rung of the ladder followed by Tim.

"Get ready to sweat, little girl," Cal bellowed, yanking on his gloves and walking to his designated side of the loft. "Don't think you got it made just cuz you got the boss on your side. Mac's spent the past month smiling at tourists and pushing paper while Tim here's been hiking mountains and building fences."

"Yep." Mac tugged a pair of gloves from his back pocket then put them on. "And Dani chopped wood last night while you drank beer and hit your cot early." He cocked an eyebrow. "So I'd say, we're pretty evenly matched."

Cal's face reddened. He ducked his head and moved to his side of the loft.

Dani turned away, her muscles stiffening as the soreness began to return. The ibuprofen Mac had given her had begun to wear off and panic clamored through her veins.

What on earth had possessed her to imagine she could pull this off? And heaven help her when Cal won. She only hoped he'd stick to his original request for a monetary bonus from Mac and didn't resort to a more ridiculous demand. Especially, one that might put her at his mercy.

She shuddered, the possibility too revolting to dwell on.

"Don't mind Cal," Mac said. "He's a good guy. Just doesn't always show it." He eased closer. "You sure you're up for this?"

Dani glanced up at Mac's low words. Taking in his concerned expression, she conjured up a smile. "Yes."

Maybe if she put everything she had into it and impressed Mac, she might still have an opportunity to persuade him to give her an hour of his time. Even if she lost.

She adjusted her gloves and slapped her hands together. A little bit of pain for the chance to seal the biggest deal Vaughn Real Estate had ever made, own this magnificent land and impress her father? It would definitely be worth it.

"We got our work cut out for us." Mac smiled. "But don't worry. Effective teamwork's as good as muscle. Would you rather toss or stack?"

She hesitated, glancing at Cal's smirking expression. "Stack."

Cal guffawed. Tim smiled and nodded encouragingly.

"All right." Mac positioned himself by the hay elevator. "Start at the corner pallet, stack the first layer of bales on edge then each one after that perpendicular to the layer below it."

"Got it." Dani took her place by the pallet and rolled her shoulders, praying her muscles would hold out on her.

"Everyone ready?" Mac asked. At their affirmations, he raised his voice above the squeak of the elevator shaft and called out, "Load 'em up."

Cheers erupted from the grounds below. Dani lifted to her toes and peeked out of the hayloft opening. A group of hands had gathered, leaning on the trailer and laughing. Mac's children whooped and jumped in front of them.

"Go, Ms. Dani!"

Jaxon, Nadine and Maddie were eagerly waiting

and watching. She smiled. All the more incentive to do well.

Dani refocused on Mac, her eyes lingering over the attractive way his jeans clung to his backside right before he spun, tossing a hay bale onto the floor at her feet.

"Heads-up." Mac's lips quirked as he jerked his chin toward the bale.

Cheeks flaming, she grabbed the bale by the rough string then heaved it onto the corner pallet. Over the next half hour, bits of hay flew through the air, grunts echoed against the rafters and the rhythmic thud of bales filled the loft. Sweat slicked her back and gnats clung to her eyelashes, stinging her eyes. A thick film of dust coated her throat.

"Tell me…again…wh—" Dani coughed, sucked in a lungful of musty air and tried again. "Tell me again why you don't just stick with the big round bales that stay in the field?"

Mac grinned as he flung another bale in her direction. "It's tradition. The way my dad used to do it. Plus, we've always had to wring every penny we can out of this place. These square bales are good backup for spoilage." He dragged an arm over his sweaty face. "A lot of customers prefer the small bales and are willing to pay more for them. Especially in a few months. They know we'll have what they need."

"On time, every time," Tim said, propping a bale against his thick thighs. "That's Mac's motto."

"Tim." Cal slapped his hat against his knee then threw it aside. "Stop your girly gabbing and move your ass."

Dani laughed. The tinge of urgency in Cal's frown put a spring in her exhausted step.

"Feeling the pressure, Cal?" she asked, heaving another bale atop her growing pile. "Sweating a bit?" She forced her sore limbs to swagger closer and lowered her voice to a manly tone. "Want to measure the height of our stacks and compare so you'll feel better?"

Mac and Tim chuckled. Cal's mouth twitched. Just a bit. Almost enough to make her think he had a genuine smile in him. But the moment passed and he scowled, instead.

"Just y'all stick to your bales and we'll stick to ours." Cal shot Tim another dirty look. "Pick up the pace, kid."

Tim laughed but resumed tossing bales. Before long, the interior of the loft darkened and thunder rumbled overhead.

"The last bale's on the way up. How many you got, Ms. Dani?"

Dani glanced up after grabbing another bale. Jaxon stood on the top rung of the ladder, arms slung around his sisters who squeezed in at his sides. He'd placed several cans of soda on the floor in front of him.

"You got enough to beat him?" Nadine asked, smile wide.

"Don't know yet," Dani said.

Muscles screaming, she heaved the bale into place then spun around for another one. The floor at her feet was empty and the rhythmic squeak of the hay elevator groaned to a halt.

"What's the verdict?" Mac called, craning his ear for the response from below.

A response was given—too faint to hear—then a

burst of laughter erupted from the hands gathered outside.

Mac straightened and smiled. "Dani won. By two bales."

The kids cheered.

Tim walked over and shook her hand. "Congratulations."

Dani's arms were so heavy she was surprised they hadn't fallen off, but Tim's firm handshake and expression of respect took the edge off her pain. "Thanks."

Cal jerked his gloves off and stalked over to the edge of the loft. "You sure you counted right, Jim?"

A deep voice cut through a clap of thunder and wave of male laughter. "Hell, yeah, I counted right."

"Ease up, Cal," Tim said, clapping him on the back. "She and Mac won fair and square."

"So, what's it gonna be?" Mac asked.

Dani stilled, studying him. Sweat trickled down his lean cheeks and his broad chest moved on heavy breaths.

"Your reward?" Mac prompted, his grin slipping. "What will it be?"

"I…" She glanced around as a heavy curtain of rain drummed the roof.

Tim smiled, grabbed a soda and ruffled Jaxon's hair. His clothes were saturated with sweat and his movements slow. Cal rubbed his forearm over his brow then shoved on his hat, trudging toward the ladder. He looked just as exhausted.

A heavy weight settled in Dani's stomach. She'd approached this task as a competition. But it was more than that for these men. It was part of a routine day of grueling work. It was tradition—just as Mac had said.

Competition aside, they'd worked just as hard as she had. And after all his sweat and heavy lifting, could she really ask Mac to sit meekly down for a sales pitch?

Legs trembling, she squeezed her eyes shut and cringed. "That overtime pay you offered earlier. Is it still on the table?"

Mac nodded. "Of course."

"Then I'll take that, please." She paused to catch her breath then gestured toward him, Tim and Cal. "Split evenly, four ways."

Tim froze, his can of soda pausing halfway toward his mouth. Cal spun to face her.

"And the rest of the afternoon off for us all," she added.

Shoulders sagging, she sat down and slumped against the stack of bales close to the edge of the loft. Rain bounced off the wood planks and a fine mist soothed the heated skin of her right arm.

"Well, I won't argue with that." Tim smiled and glanced at Mac. "Storm's settling in. Want me and Jim to give the kids a ride back to the lodge? Then come back for you two?"

"That'd be great," Mac said. "Thanks."

"You're staying for lunch, aren't you, Ms. Dani?" Jaxon lifted onto his toes and peered at her expectantly.

She grinned. "Lunch would be great."

Excitement lighting their faces, Jaxon and Nadine bounced back down the ladder. Maddie, oddly subdued, followed at a slower pace.

Dani watched as Cal stepped onto the ladder then hesitated. His eyes met hers, the deep grooves fanning from the corners drawing up as they narrowed.

"We make a pretty good team when we're moving in the same direction," Dani said softly. "Don't you agree?"

He stared at her then tapped his hat more firmly on his head as he descended the ladder. "Ma'am."

Dani sighed and closed her eyes, the sound of Cal and Tim's steps fading as they left. Moments later, something cold nudged the back of her hand.

"Here," Mac said, pressing a can of soda in her palm. "You've earned it."

She smiled. "What? No beer?"

Mac chuckled and eased down beside her. "Not this time of day. It's tra—"

"—dition?" Dani popped the top on the can and breathed in the sugary mist appreciatively before taking a deep swallow. "Another one of your father's rules?"

"Yep. Never let any hay go to waste, work until the sun hits the horizon and no liquor 'til the moon shines."

Dani rolled another swig of soda around her mouth and stared at his big boots resting beside her scuffed sneakers. His muscular arm, warm and solid, brushed against hers as he lifted his can, spreading pleasurable tingles over her skin.

"But you're giving us the afternoon off." She tilted her head back and looked up at him. "Isn't that breaking one of the rules?"

"Depends on how you look at it." He waved his tanned hand toward the steady fall of rain outside the loft. "I don't see any sun out there right now. Do you?"

She shook her head, her eyes straying to the strong curve of his stubble-lined jaw. "But…could you ever see yourself breaking tradition if there was a good enough reason? Like if…"

She hesitated, carefully weighing phrases. *If it eased your workload? If it brought in more money than you'd ever imagined? Enabled you to spend all the time you wanted with your son?*

"Say there was an opportunity for growth here at the ranch," she said. "One that required you to do things differently than how your father pictured them. Would you do it?"

He stayed silent, watching the rain ricochet off the wood planks at her side. His eyes moved to the droplets collecting on her arm then drifted up to her face. "I don't know." His scrutiny warmed her cheeks. "I guess it'd depend."

"On what?"

He frowned. "The circumstances. How much the changes would conflict with my father's vision for the place. This is my family home. My childhood memories, the life I want for my kids—my way of life—is embedded in this land. I'd never do anything to jeopardize that."

"But what if the changes brought new traditions? And new opportunities?"

His eyes narrowed. "Why are you asking?"

Oh, no. She was doing it anyway. She was sitting Mac down and grilling him just like a Vaughn Real Estate agent. Just like she'd decided not to.

Dani shrank back then stuck her flaming face out the loft's opening. The soft rumble of thunder and sharp lick of rain against her cheeks drowned out the whisper of guilt lurking in the back of her mind. And the cool trickle of water over her neck, soaking into her collar, stilled her nerves.

"I shouldn't have pried." She settled back against the hay bales, licking the tangy taste of rainwater from her lips. "I'm sorry."

Mac's expression softened and he grinned. His big

hand lifted and his callused thumb brushed a drop of water from the corner of her mouth, sending a streak of heat through her chest. "You're apologizing? Again?"

She leaned into his light touch, laughing softly. "Yes. I'm sorry. Again."

"Sorry enough to stay and help me out?" His face flushed as the soft words escaped him and he seemed to visibly shake himself. "I mean…" He lowered his hand abruptly and cleared his throat. "My original offer still stands. It'd be strictly business. I've been itching to get some new blood on my team. Someone with energy and drive. And if you took the job, what goes on here would become your business, too. You could ask all the questions you want."

She stilled, her mind whirling.

…what goes on here would become your business.

…you could ask all the questions you want.

All of it at Mac's request.

What harm would it do, really? If she stayed just for a few days? She could help lighten Mac's workload, get the information needed to draw up a successful plan for improvements and maybe even change Mac's mind about selling his land.

It was a stretch, sure. But it eased her conscience a bit to know that Mac was the one inviting her into his business. It would save her from returning to the boardroom empty-handed and from becoming a complete disappointment in her father's eyes.

As long as she kept her focus on the deal and not… Mac.

"Okay," she whispered. "I'll stay for a few days. See how things go."

"Thank you." Mac smiled, looked past her to the

field below then shoved to his feet. "Tim made it back with the truck." He eyed her sprawled frame. "Need a hand getting up?"

"No, thanks." She forced a smile, ignoring the painful burn on her skin and deep within her muscles. "I can manage."

"You sure?" Mac smirked. "You gotta be as sore as all get-out by now."

"Nope. I'm fine."

She grabbed the edge of a bale and pulled but her thighs locked up, threatening to give out.

Mac laughed then thrust out a hand. "You're a bad liar."

Dani's chest tightened as she slowly put her hand in his. That was exactly what she used to think, too. But the shameful fact was, she was a lot better at lying than she'd thought.

Chapter Four

"What do you mean you haven't made the sale? You've been in Elk Valley for two weeks now."

Dani squinted her eyes against the afternoon sun and clutched her cell phone tighter to her ear. Even though Scott was her younger brother, he was no less demanding as her boss. And the few days she'd promised to work for Mac had lengthened into a much longer stay.

"I've been..."

Falling off horses. Backing tractors into fences. Consistently running Mac's patience into the ground. That was in addition to the times she'd been distracted by Mac's smile or the sexy rumble of his voice. And it didn't include all the times her fumbling on the job had frustrated Cal or disappointed Tim. Her inept actions had squandered just about every bit of respect she'd earned winning that hay bet.

She shoved her fist in her pocket and leaned back against the stable wall. "Working. I've been surveying the property, adding up renovation costs, sketching plans—"

"Wait a minute. Mac Tenley, the most hard-headed

throwback in existence, actually granted you access to his land?"

"He's not a throwback."

Dani bit her lip, halting her sharp response, and peeked around the side of the stable.

Mac stood across the field, talking to Nadine and Maddie while Jaxon pounded his baseball in his glove. The grounds were still quiet save for a few guests gathering in a neighboring field for an afternoon hike and another group preparing for a trail ride in one of the paddocks.

Thank goodness. She'd practically swallowed her lunch whole then slipped off for the rest of her break in order to speak with Scott privately.

Dani ducked back behind the stable. "Mac's just big on tradition," she continued. "And yes. I'm staying in one of the cabins."

"You're *staying* there? And Tenley's okay with that?"

Her throat tightened as her next words slipped right past her lips. "He invited me."

Scott whistled low and slow. "Damn. That's more than anyone else has managed. Something you said must've turned his head."

Dani clamped her mouth shut. She studied a sole cloud drifting across the blue sky just above the mountain peak. Listened to the rustling movements of a small animal in a nearby tree.

"What *did* you say?" Scott asked.

She looked down. Picked at the mud caked under a chipped fingernail. "I just said that I was here to help." *Good.* That was partially true. "That I needed to be here."

Another bit of truth.

"And that you were dead-set on becoming the new owner of his prized possession?" Scott pressed.

"Of course." Dani winced. *Another big. Fat. Lie.* This had become a horrible habit. "Just not in so many words. And maybe, not exactly...like that."

"Uh-huh." Scott's tone tightened. "What are you doing, Dani?"

She straightened, the rough wood of the stable walls digging into her back, voice hardening. "My job."

A swift pull of breath and the squeak of a door crossed the line. Muffled voices and sporadic honking filled the background then another deep drag of air rattled through the receiver.

"Are you out back smoking again?" Dani asked.

"Maybe."

A smile tugged at her mouth. "That's not good for you."

Scott laughed. "Neither is stress but I'm still in the Vaughn high-rise." He sighed. "Look. Whatever plans you're drawing up can be made here. I know we've taken advantage of a few loopholes in the past but we've always operated aboveboard—*in an honest way.* You're great at what you do but you're in over your head with this one. I know you feel pressure to make this deal and I know how difficult things have been for you recently—"

"Difficult?" Dani shoved off the stable, flinching as a splinter lodged in her palm. "I worked my fingers to the bone for almost a decade, interning at ungodly hours, squeezing in two college degrees and doing more time in an entry-level position than anyone else at the company, just so my boss could banish me to a corner and toss everything I earned to my little broth—"

She stopped, remorse swamping her.

"I didn't ask for the promotion," Scott said softly. "I would never do that to you, Dani. Not ever."

Dani swallowed hard. "I know. And I didn't mean it that way. I really didn't. Please forgive me."

"For what?"

"For doing to you what you'd never do to me." A humorless laugh burst from her. "Because that's what I'm doing, isn't it? Trying to pluck that position out from under you?"

"You've earned it, just like you said." His words turned hesitant. "He misses you."

Dad? She doubted it. He was probably poring over a dozen contracts as she spoke. "Then why hasn't he called? Told me himself?"

"Is that why you've stayed down there for so long?" Scott asked. "To see if he would?"

"No." Something thudded in the distance, echoing across the field. She stepped further behind the stable. "Not at all."

"Then why are you still there?"

"Because I really do want to help," she said. That, at least, was completely true. "Did you know Mac has three kids? And that he's a widower?"

Scott groaned softly. "That has nothing to do with this deal. It's business. Not personal. You're getting too personal with Tenley—"

"No, I'm not," she said. "Besides, it's not just Mac I want to help. I want to help Dad out by making the deal and I want to ensure this land is acquired by people who will preserve and take care of it. We'd protect it better than our competitors."

A low-hanging branch on the tree next to her wavered and a chipmunk sprang from the leaves then plopped onto the ground. He looked up at her and froze, his tiny ears pinned back and cheeks packed solid with treats, before darting off into the brush.

Dani grinned. "It's beautiful here. No one can deny what a treasure this place is and it's worth whatever price Mac asks. It's perfect for escaping corporate stress. You'd love it, Scott."

He blew out a breath. "Peaceful rest surrounded by nothing but mountains? I'd probably stay longer than you have." His tone deepened. "But if you want to help Tenley, you need to make the sale now. One of the agents reported yesterday that a bank contact assured him two months—three at the most—is all that stands between that property and foreclosure. If the right agency holds their hand and places their bets right, that land will be bought with pennies."

Heart stalling, she tightened her grip around the phone. "And Mac will walk away with nothing."

"Yes." Scott cleared his throat. "You're one of my best agents and I need you here. Keep it professional, close the deal and come home. That's a direct order from your boss." His voice softened. "And a sincere request from your little brother. Dad's not the only one that misses you, Dani."

"Ms. Dani!"

She jumped, fumbling for the phone as it slipped from her fingers. Jaxon ran around the corner, breathing hard.

"The horses got out." He doubled over, hands on his

knees, as he struggled to catch his breath. "Mr. Tim said to come help."

Dani dashed to the front of the stable, managing a quick "I've got to go" to Scott before shoving the phone back into her pocket. She drew up short at the edge of the field.

The far end of the fencing—the one she'd backed into with the tractor yesterday—had toppled over, leaving a gaping hole behind. All eight horses, previously grazing in the field, had galloped away, the last one trotting off with a tail swish toward a nearby mountain trail.

"Did you patch that corner you knocked out like I asked you to?" Cal shouted over his shoulder, running toward the stable.

"Of course, I did." She followed him then grabbed ropes off wall hooks at his direction.

"Well, obviously, you didn't do it well enough." Cal thrust more ropes into her hands then started running back toward the field. "Get the lead out, girl, and take those to Mac and Tim."

She did, tearing across the deep grass and dirt paths as fast as her legs would carry her. Jaxon kept close to her heels.

"I'll take 'em," Mac called out from astride one of the fastest horses, expression dark with frustration, his muscular arm stretching out for the ropes.

Dani handed them over. "I'm sorry, Mac. The fence seemed solid when I finished last night."

"Not solid enough," he bit out. "It's gonna be hell rounding 'em up before dark."

She lowered her head, the disappointment in his face sending a fresh wave of heat up her neck.

"I'm coming with you." Jaxon sprang toward one of the horses already saddled for a trail ride.

"No, Jaxon." Mac tossed the ropes to Tim and two other hands who passed by on their mounts and galloped off in the direction of the escaped horses. "Stay here and watch your sisters."

Jaxon scowled, eyeing Nadine and Maddie as they stood watching from the other side of the fence. "But I want to go with you and help."

"Not gonna happen," Mac said firmly, nudging his horse toward the mountain trail. He glanced back at Dani. "Let the guests know the trail ride and hike for today are canceled. Tell 'em they'll get a refund. Then untack the rest of the horses and stable them."

Chest aching, Dani nodded then watched as he rode off, arms hanging helplessly at her sides.

"Great. Now it'll be forever before he comes back."

Dani looked down. Maddie stopped by her side, crossed her arms and frowned as Mac disappeared into the woods.

"It won't be forever," Nadine said, jogging up behind her sister. "Dad's the fastest rider here. He'll catch 'em."

"Yeah." Maddie's frown deepened. "But he's gotta find them first. And that part will take forever." Her green eyes flashed up at Dani. "He was s'posed to take us to the creek later. Bet we won't get to go now. I wish you would've fixed the fence better."

Dani squirmed. Funny how a few honest words from a child could make you feel two feet tall. She should've been doing her job, not lying and sneaking off for secret phone calls.

Mac had hired her to ease his workload. Yet, here she was, steadily adding to it.

"I'm sorry, Maddie." Dani shook her head and sighed. "I know you were looking forward to spending time with him."

"It ain't your fault, Ms. Dani," Jaxon said. "He was supposed to take me fishing this morning and that didn't work out, either. That's just how it goes around here." He jerked his chin toward the antsy group of guests, grumbling their displeasure by the fence. "Want me to tell 'em about the trail ride and hike?"

"No, thank you, Jaxon." Dani sucked in a deep breath and headed in that direction. "I'm the one that messed up. I'll take care of it."

There were thirteen guests in all. After informing them the afternoon activities had been canceled and that refunds would be issued, Dani was left standing with only seven.

"I didn't drive all the way from Florida just to sit in a run-down room and stare at the wall," a man grumped, shoving his gray hair more firmly under his cap. "Wouldn't be so dang bad if we had cable. Or Wi-Fi. Or anything resembling modern amenities. Did you know only one of the outlets in our room actually works? My wife and I have to take turns charging our cell phones." He harrumphed, straightened the belt on his jeans then started for the lodge. "Come on, Lou Ann. We're getting out of here. It'll be worth driving an hour just to find a hotel with dependable electricity."

"But, sir…" Dani leaned heavily on the fence, the sun-heated wood searing her skin as she watched him walk away.

Make that five. There were now five guests left.

She'd run half of Mac's guests off in less than one day and there was no telling how much money she'd caused him to lose.

A soft palm patted the back of her hand. "Don't mind him, dear. Harold's just disappointed that he won't get to ride a horse today." An older woman with a kind voice leaned closer. "He bought brand-new jeans and a pair of boots just for the occasion." She smiled. "And he's been missing his baseball games the past two days on account of the TV not working. He likes the Marlins and they're playing Cincinnati today."

"The Braves, Lou Ann." Harold stopped and spun around, stressing, "The Marlins are playing the Braves. One of their biggest rivals and I'm going to miss it."

"What if I could guarantee you an uninterrupted viewing of the game?" Dani rushed out. "And a free trail ride as soon as possible? Would you give us one more chance?"

He shifted from one foot to the other, eyeing his wife. "Well..."

"The TV in the lounge works," Jaxon said. He ducked between the fence rungs and walked over to Harold. "You could watch it with me."

"And it's connected to a deck with a great view," Dani added. "I'll open up the windows and doors for some fresh, mountain air and arrange for snacks and anything else that would make it more enjoyable."

"I do like the peace and quiet here, Harold," Lou Ann said. "And you can't beat the scenery from that lodge. We won't be able to watch the sun set behind those beautiful mountains in a hotel room."

Oh, please, please, take the offer and don't let me

disappoint Mac more than I already have. Dani held her breath as Harold studied her.

"All right." Harold looked down at Jaxon then nodded. "We'll give it one more try. But I want that horse ride soon."

"Of course." Dani smiled gratefully at Lou Ann, high-fived Jaxon then led the way to the lodge. "One baseball game coming up. Anyone else that would like to join in, please follow me."

Every guest—back up to seven now, thankfully—followed and twenty minutes later, they were all seated in front of the TV, baseball game on and snacks in hand. Jaxon, armed with two sodas, sat beside Harold on the couch and offered him one.

Harold smiled. "Thank you, son."

"Anything else I can get you?" Dani asked.

He shook his head. "This helps tremendously. Thank you…er…"

"Dani," she said. "We want you to enjoy your stay and I'm glad I could help."

She straightened, pride surging through her veins as she smiled at Jaxon, who chatted about baseball with Harold. Then she laughed as Nadine and Maddie smiled and munched strawberries with Lou Ann, fresh juice dribbling down their chins, their disappointments forgotten.

This little taste of success was richer than any she'd experienced in New York. But her smile fell at the thought of Mac riding hard through mountain trails, tracking down horses she'd failed to keep watch over and the conflicting emotions warring within her chest made it clear that Scott had been right in at least one respect.

She was making this personal.

Dani eased away, returned to the paddock and began untacking the horses. Her hands stilled over a mare's mane, her fingers threading through the thick strands.

There was no way around it. This land was too precious to allow it to fall into negligent hands and the only way any of this would play in Mac's favor was if she persuaded him to sell now—even if it left her looking like a villain in his eyes.

Keep it professional, close the deal and come home.

Dani patted the mare's neck then pressed her forehead to the horse's smooth hide. It was time to tell Mac the truth.

"Whoa." Mac pulled gently on the reins, bringing the mare beneath him to a stop, then cast one more glance at the empty trail behind him.

"Wanna take one more look?"

Mac faced Tim and shook his head. "No. It's getting dark."

"There's still some light left," Tim said, tugging the mare he led to a stop beside his mount. "I can put this girl to bed then come back out and make one more round. That little bastard's bound to be 'round here somewhere."

Mac grunted. *Little bastard* was right. Standing at only 15 hands, Bullet made up for his small stature with plenty of speed. The roan gelding was hard to catch in a fenced paddock much less roaming freely with a head start.

"Nah," Mac said. "Bullet's long gone by now."

Along with the three and a half grand he'd planned to make off the gelding's sell. Not only was he going to lose the much-needed cash to make a back payment on the ranch but he was probably going to lose future business from the couple interested, as well.

Who'd buy horses from a man who couldn't even guarantee they'd be there the day you came to pick them up? And worse, who'd bother doing business with you at all when there was a damn good chance your business would foreclose in a month or two?

At least, that was what Jim Reid had predicted last week when Mac had gone hat-in-hand to the bank for another extension on his loan payments, only to be denied. And that was after he'd had to endure a half-hour "told you so" session rife with platitudes from the older man.

"Told you not to hire that gal," Cal shouted from the bottom of the trail. "Every problem we've had the past two weeks boils down to that ditzy chick—"

"I didn't ask for your opinion, Cal, and I'll run this place as I see fit. You don't like it, you're free to leave." Mac kicked his horse's flanks and galloped past him. "Now, move your ass. You got work to do."

He urged the mare faster when he hit the valley, the hot wind whipping his face and the heavy pound of the horse's powerful stride beating rhythmically through his frame. The hard ride shook some of the pressing weight from his shoulders and rattled loose thoughts he'd locked away years ago. The ones that burned his skin and punched another guilty hole in his chest every time they materialized.

Where would he be now if he'd chosen a different path? If he hadn't spent the past ten years trying to re-suscitate his parents' dead business? If he and Nicole had been more careful and not gotten pregnant then married at eighteen—

Mac jerked the reins, bringing the mare to a halt and hanging his head. *You wouldn't have Jaxon, you selfish sonofabitch. You wouldn't have Maddie or Nadine. And you wouldn't have had seven good years of marriage with Nicole.*

There was no place in his life—or heart—for such weak, regretful thoughts. They were a betrayal to Nicole and his children.

The steady pounding of a hammer brought his head up, his eyes roving over the green pastures and settling on Dani. She bent beside the broken fence, a hammer in one hand as she struggled to balance a wood beam on her hip and nail it home simultaneously.

It slipped from her grip, banged against her knee then thudded to the ground. The colorful words she spat echoed across the valley and coaxed a smile to his lips.

Damn, she was cute. Feisty. Prideful. Hardheaded, too. And she had the most tempting curves he'd ever seen...

He peeled his attention away from the soft swell of her bottom and reminded himself that he shouldn't notice. Matter of fact, he'd tried his best not to notice over the past two weeks. He'd tried to put his energy into training her instead of admiring her, but there were just so many things about her that he had trouble looking away from.

Like the way the tip of her tongue touched the corner of her mouth when she concentrated on something. Or the way her ponytail swished across her back when she stomped away from one of Cal's fussing fits. Hell, that shiny swath of hair had as much attitude as she did.

And her laugh…*ah, man*. That sexy laugh of hers made his stomach tighten. Made him want to tug her close, feel her chest vibrate against his and her soft breaths sweep across his skin. Made him feel as though…

Maybe that's what it is. She made him feel. She reminded him there was a world outside of Elk Valley. One he'd grown brash enough to roam eleven years ago with or without Nicole. Right after his high school graduation ceremony, he'd told his twin brother, Nate, that he was joining him on the rodeo circuit then he'd packed his bags, planning to leave the next morning.

But that was before Nicole had told him about Jaxon. Afterward, that'd been the end of that.

"Anything else you want us to do after we brush the horses down and turn 'em in for the night?"

Mac shifted his attention to Cal who walked his horse slowly past, Tim and the recovered horses trailing behind. Cal's head was tilted down and his voice was meek. As far as apologies went, that was the best Mac had ever seen from Cal.

"No." Mac dismounted. "Take care of Willow, too, then y'all can knock off for the day."

Cal clicked his tongue and Willow followed the rest of the horses to the stable.

Mac made his way over to Dani. She stood, clutched the beam against her hip and glared at the broken fence.

"Want some help?"

She looked up, the rosy flush in her cheeks and wisps of hair clinging to her sweaty forehead making him grin. "I could use it." She shrugged. "That is, if you feel like helping the person that cost you a stack of cash and ran your guests off."

He frowned and glanced toward the lodge. The sun began to set, casting a bright orange glow over the empty grounds. "They all left?"

"Half of them." She dragged her forearm across her face. "I bribed the rest of them with a baseball game on TV, then Ann closed the office and took made-to-order requests for dinner. They're in the dining room eating now."

"Kids, too?"

She nodded, smiling a little. "Jaxon helped the girls get washed up and seated. They requested a big fat cheese pizza for dinner."

Mac chuckled. His girls might be small but they could put a grown man to shame when it came to scarfing down a pizza. "Well, since that's well in hand, I say we get to hammering."

He grabbed the hammer and a nail off the ground, squatted then motioned for her to put the beam into position. She did so, kneeling at his side and holding it in place.

"I'm really sorry, Mac." Her words were muffled. "I thought I'd repaired it strong enough."

Pausing, he glanced down and nudged her with his elbow. "You didn't do it on purpose. It was a mistake. That's all. You're entitled to your fair share."

She lifted her chin from her chest, her ivory cheeks flushing. "Did you find all of the horses?"

"All but one." He hammered the nail until it hit home then added another for extra insurance. "Bullet's still gallivanting around the mountains. He gets bored quick. I'd bet my last dime he's the one that kicked out this loose fence."

He tossed two more nails in his palm then moved to the other end of the beam, his thigh pressing against Dani's as he squatted again. His quad tightened, a pleasurable sensation moving through him, and he shifted closer.

"And are you?" she asked.

"Am I what?"

"Betting your last dime?"

He froze. "I'm making do."

Jim Reid flashed through his mind, the older man's wrinkle-free suit and smug smile facing him from behind a mahogany desk. *I told you to sell four years ago, Mac. A savvy businessman would have had trouble propping that place back on its feet, much less a widower with three children. Now, you'll be lucky to walk out of there with a shirt on your back.*

Mac gritted his teeth, positioned the nail tight with his fingertips then hammered. "I always make do."

"But without customers…" Her soft voice firmed. "Today was my fault. I caused you to lose six paying guests. But there weren't many more than that to begin with and there hasn't been since I've been here." Her hands shifted on the beam, knuckles whitening as her grip tightened. "I know someone who could help you. Someone who could turn this place around, keep it from shutting down and make you more money than you'd ever be able to spend."

"Someone in New York?" He hammered harder, cutting glances at her shapely arms. At the way the pounds of the hammer shook them.

"Yes." She wrapped her arms around the fence and

raised her voice over the pounding. "I know you're against it, but maybe it's time to reconsider selling."

"Why? So some fool can traipse in here and deform the place? Turn it into one of those dime-a-dozen tourist traps?" He slammed the nail home then threw the hammer into the grass. "What the hell would some stranger know about how my parents worked their fingers to the bone raising this ranch from nothing but rock and soil? What would they know about protecting the serenity and dignity of these mountains? About what this valley needs to breathe? To thrive?"

She hugged the fence closer, a wary expression crossing her delicate features.

"I won't sell out—no matter how much I stand to make—and I don't want to hand this place over to someone else."

Voice shaking, she asked, "Then what *do* you want, Mac?"

He dug his fists into his knees. "I just want to be able to pay my bills long enough to pass this land on to my kids. I want the time to help them enjoy it. I want to be able to talk to them without having to walk away midsentence. Look them in the face instead of over my shoulder—" His voice cracked and he swallowed hard, choking back the emotions strangling him. "I could've left Elk Valley years ago like my brother. Could've just shoved this place off to some developer and hauled ass. But I didn't. I stayed and worked. And I'll continue to do so until those greedy bastards come in here and force me out."

Her chin trembled and those blue eyes of hers, wounded, glistened up at him, a tear clinging to her thick lashes. That tiny drop kicked him hard in the gut and the fight bled right out of him.

"Please don't look at me like that."

A puzzled light entered her eyes.

"Like you feel sorry for me." He cleared his throat, softening his gruff voice and leaning closer. "Like I disappointed you. I didn't mean to go off on you like that."

She smiled, small and sad, then slowly unwound her arms from the fence. Her soft palm cupped his jaw. "It'd be hard for a man like you to disappoint me. Or any woman, for that matter. And to be honest…" Her voice faded to a whisper, flush deepening, as her attention drifted to his mouth. "Sorry isn't exactly what I'm feeling right now."

Heaven help him, her sweet words were so soothing and solid. He wanted to lean on them. Lean on *her*.

The sun dipped, the last rays of light pooling softly over the gentle curve of her cheek and pink, parted lips. Everything about her pulling him in.

Mac dipped his head and kissed her. Right there in the middle of the valley.

As his mouth moved over hers, the sky slowly darkened and the humid air of the day gave way to a refreshing night breeze. The taste of her, sweet and clean, washed over him, coaxing his arms around her, one hand splaying low over her back and the other caressing the nape of her neck. He dove deeper, nudging her lips further apart with his, then swept his tongue in to savor her.

God, it'd been so long since he'd held a woman. Kissed her.

Dani met each of his movements with her own, angling her head, slim fingers kneading his shoulders and chest as she pressed closer, causing his blood to rush.

He struggled to slow down and keep his hands from roaming further. He'd forgotten how exciting it was to be touched and tempted. And he wished he was free to explore more. Wished he could stretch out and hold her against him. Wished he wasn't—

He jerked his mouth from hers, his heart thudding against his ribs. "Dani, I…" Breathing hard, he released her gently then glanced around. The dim lights of the lodge didn't reach the empty expanse of land around them and, thankfully, the kids were still inside. "I didn't intend to do that. I was out of line. I promised I'd keep this strictly business."

She blinked then drew back, her expression dazed as her fingertips touched the moist, reddened curve of her bottom lip. "But it felt…"

Fantastic.

The thought hit Mac the same time the unspoken sentiment gleamed in her eyes. But so did the reality of what he was doing: taking advantage of an employee. Sacrificing time he should be spending with his kids in favor of holding a woman.

But not just any woman—*Dani*. Beautiful and strong. Prideful but giving. Honest and hard-working. The only woman in the past four years who'd slipped under his skin and pulled his focus from his family.

His chest tightened. "I should go in." He forced himself to his feet then helped her up. "I need to get a head start on cleaning the rooms in the lodge so I'll have some time with Jaxon and the girls tonight."

She gripped his wrists, stopping his hands from leaving her altogether. "Why don't you let me do that?

It's my fault your guests left. And tomorrow, why don't you take the day off? With Cal and Tim's help, I can manage things around here and I promise not to cause any more trouble. That way, you can spend tonight and tomorrow with your children."

Mac hesitated, her concerned expression making him want to tug her close and cover her mouth with his again. Instead, he sighed and shook his head. "That's nice of you to offer but I can't afford to take a day off."

Her lips twisted. "Thanks to me, you have six fewer guests so there's a lot less work to worry about. Go ahead and take the day. I can manage." She released him, averting her eyes and mumbling, "I owe you that, at least."

He grinned, not doubting for a second that Dani could hold her own, even when things didn't go as planned. But he hated the thought of her feeling indebted to him.

And he had a nagging need to touch her silky skin just once more.

"Hey." He nudged her chin up with a knuckle then drifted the back of his hand across her smooth cheek. It was soft and warm. Like the rest of her. "You don't owe me anything," he whispered. "But I will take you up on your offer. I could take Jaxon hiking in the morning. That'd give me some time alone with him, if you wouldn't mind watching the girls for the first half of the day?"

Dani nodded, her attention drifting back to his mouth.

He smiled. An excited relief at the prospect of an unimpeded day with his children mingled with the intoxicating buzz of attraction in his veins. "Thank you."

She didn't smile back and he could barely make out her low words as she walked away, her slender figure fading across the darkened field.

"Don't thank me yet."

Chapter Five

Sorry isn't exactly what I'm feeling right now.

Dani hefted a potted azalea out of the truck bed and set it on the ground in front of the stable, trying her best to figure out what she *did* feel after that spectacular kiss from Mac last night.

Sympathy? Of course. That was no surprise. She knew firsthand what it was like to be brushed aside as though hard work didn't matter, and she'd sympathize with anyone fighting to succeed professionally. But losing Elk Valley Ranch wasn't just a professional concern for Mac—it was personal, too.

And the feeling that sprang up when he'd kissed her hadn't just been professional, it had been...

She nudged the potted plant in line with the dozen others then straightened, squinting against the early morning sun and admiring how it glistened over the thick, dewy grass. Admiration. That was what that feeling had been. She admired his work ethic and devotion to his children. Any woman would melt over that.

Closing her eyes, she stifled a groan. If only that was the main reason she'd melted in his arms last night. No, she'd felt something entirely different the second Mac's warm mouth had claimed hers—good old-fashioned lust.

Except it wasn't just good, it was great. And it wasn't old-fashioned, either. She'd never felt anything that intense in her past relationships, which had been few and far between. She'd never felt that soft stirring in her chest and persistent tug in her belly before. And she'd definitely never gone to sleep with a man on her mind and woken to the thought of him first thing the next morning.

That was the most troubling thing about that kiss—wanting more. But the most humiliating part of it was that she'd never actually summoned up the courage to tell him the truth before or after. Something she should have already done.

Throat tightening, she shoved her hands in her pockets and studied the ants trailing across the dirt. What a mess she gotten herself into. *What a big—*

"Having second thoughts?"

Dani glanced up, the grin on Mac's handsome face making her catch her breath. Her eyes strayed over his muscular frame as he approached, noting the same hint of heated interest from last night still gleamed in his expression as he watched her. He drew to a halt and his strong hands flexed at his sides. The same ones that had roved eagerly over her neck and back last night, gently touching and holding.

What a big, beautiful man—

Oh, boy. She was in more trouble than she'd initially thought.

"No." She jerked her hands from her pockets, ripped her attention away from him and focused on Jaxon and the girls as they chased each other on the other side of the field. "I'm happy to help."

"So you say." Mac's grin grew. He glanced over his shoulder at his kids before leaning in to whisper, "But my girls can be a handful."

"Not a problem." Fixated on the delicious throb of his low voice, she eased nearer and whispered back, "I may have never babysat before, but teenagers half my age do it all the time. So how hard could it be?"

He laughed, green eyes sparkling down at her. "You'd be surprised."

"Even so, I'm well-equipped to handle them." She smiled and tapped his broad chest with a finger. "I can be a handful myself, in case you haven't noticed."

His laughter faded. He studied her from head to toe, his approving eyes sending exciting shivers over each inch of skin he perused. "Oh, I've noticed."

She locked her knees against the slight quiver in her thighs, afraid she'd melt into a puddle at his feet. He shifted closer, the front of his T-shirt brushing against hers and the pads of his fingers caressing her elbow.

"What're y'all whispering about?"

They sprang apart.

Maddie stood a couple of feet behind Mac, frowning, and waiting for an answer. Nadine and Jaxon stood at their sister's side, nodding at each other with smug grins.

"Nothing." Dani stumbled back a few more steps and looked away as Mac dragged a hand over the back of his neck. "We were just…"

"Discussing how you and Nadine are going to be on your best behavior while Jaxon and I are gone." Mac squatted in front of Maddie and took her hands in his.

"I'll be back before you know it, then I'll take you and Nadine up to the creek."

"Why can't we go with you and Jaxon?" Maddie asked.

"Because we're hiking to the overlook and it's a long, dangerous trek up there." Mac kissed her forehead then stood, motioning toward the azaleas nearby. "And from the looks of things, I think Ms. Dani has something fun planned for you."

Dani hesitated as Maddie stared at the plants. "I talked your dad into letting me plant some flowers around the stable this morning and Mr. Tim drove me to a nursery to pick up a few while you had breakfast. They're azaleas. Do you like them?"

"I like 'em," Nadine said, bounding over then dragging a shovel off the truck bed. "Do we get to dig holes for them?"

"Yes." Dani laughed and helped her lower the shovel to the ground. "You can dig as many holes as you'd like." She turned to Maddie. "Maddie, I thought you could help me pack them in with potting soil? Or you could spread the pine straw if you'd prefer?"

Maddie stood still for a moment, winding her pink hair ribbon around her pointer finger, then walked slowly toward the plants. She touched one of the delicate petals and grinned. "I like the pink ones."

Dani smiled and blew out a small breath. "I thought you might. I picked those out just for you."

Maddie's smile grew bigger. "Thank you."

"You're welcome."

"Sounds like you have everything well in hand." Mac winked.

She nodded, pleasure stirring in her veins while she

tried not to stare at his handsome face too long. "You don't have to worry about a thing."

Mac kissed Nadine on the cheek then nudged Jaxon toward the hiking path. "Come on. Let's get going."

"Bye, Ms. Dani," Jaxon called out, striding away with his father.

Dani waved back then pulled her attention from Mac's powerful frame and caught Maddie's eyes on her. *Great.* It was bad enough she'd lied to Mac, but admiring his physique in front of his children elevated her misdeeds to another level.

Nervously, she clapped her hands then rubbed them together briskly. "So. Why don't we get started?"

One hour later, Dani knelt beside a freshly planted azalea and admired Maddie and Nadine's handiwork. "Nadine, you judged the depth of this hole just right. And, Maddie, you spread the pine straw perfectly."

"Thanks!"

Whether out of habit or coincidence, the girls chimed their response in unison then plopped onto their butts beside the plant and giggled at each other. Their snaggletooth grins and shared amusement made Dani chuckle. The morning task may have started out rocky but it had quickly become fun for all of them.

She patted the thick stack of straw then sat beside them, then tilted her head back and looked up at the sky. A heavy cluster of clouds covered the sun and a steady breeze swept across the valley. The air was still sticky and humid but the rush of wind against sweat-slicked skin was a blessed relief.

"Looks like one of those summer storms your father talks about might show up soon." Dani smiled. Sweat rolled down her back, tickling her skin. She scratched at it. "A nice, heavy rain right after we finish planting is exactly what these flowers need."

A hand caught hold of hers in midscratch and tugged. "You paint your nails?" Maddie asked, tilting Dani's fingers this way and that against her bare knee.

"Yes, though they look worse for the wear right now," Dani answered. She frowned at the chipped polish then lifted her other hand toward Maddie, fingers spread. "These are in better shape." She laughed. "Most likely because I tend to shovel manure with my right hand more than my left."

Maddie glanced up at her beneath her lashes, nibbling on her lower lip, then smoothed her fingertips over the intact nail polish of Dani's pointer finger. "It's pink," she whispered. "Like my mama's."

Dani stilled. She cast a quick glance at Nadine who sat quietly at her sister's side, staring at the nail, too. Their smiles had faded. "Did she ever paint yours?" she asked Maddie softly.

"I don't remember." Maddie released Dani's hand then grabbed her long, hair ribbon and rubbed the silky material between her fingers. "But she liked pink." She looked up and smiled. A real one. "Just like me. I know because this was hers, too," she added, tugging on her ribbon. "Dad gave it to me. And he gave us lots of her nail polish and most of it's pink." She turned to her sister. "Isn't that right?"

Nadine nodded. "Yeah. But she had others. Like red and—"

"But pink was her favorite. She always had it on in her pictures." Maddie spun back to Dani. "And she liked roasting marshmallows. I know that, too, because my dad told me that was her favorite thing to do when they went camping." She twisted her hands in her lap, her words strained. "He misses her you know? He says so all the time."

Nadine drew her knees to her chest and rested her chin on them. "I wish we remembered her better."

Dani's throat tightened. "I know what you mean. I lost my mother a long time ago, so I don't remember everything about her." She glanced at Maddie. "But talking about what I do remember always helps."

Maddie smiled a little. "Dad said she used to braid our hair every night."

Nadine held up a tangled section of her hair and laughed. "So we wouldn't have so many of these."

Dani managed a small smile in return. Polished nails, silky hair ribbons, braids. Camping and roasting marshmallows. Judging from the two pretty girls sitting beside her, their mother—Nicole, if she recalled correctly—had probably been beautiful. She must have been a wonderful woman. Had to have been in order to earn Mac's devotion and raise three gorgeous children.

It all sounded like a sweet dream. One Mac and his children had cruelly lost. One Nicole had lost, as well.

"She sounds like she was a fantastic mom," Dani whispered, smoothing a hand through Maddie's long hair. She blinked back a tear as Maddie leaned into her touch, snuggling against her. "I'm so sorry you lost her. I'm sure she loved you girls very much and would be so proud of you now."

Dani held Maddie close, sympathetic sorrow filling her and spurring a sincere wish that the girls and Jaxon still had their mother. And—as much as it burned her chest—that Mac still had his wife.

"I imagine your dad loved your mother very much, too."

Maddie stiffened against her then pulled away. "Yeah." Her voice hardened as she examined Dani's face. "He did. And he said he always would."

Dani froze, heart aching at the sadness and anger darkening Maddie's eyes.

"You like him, don't you?" Maddie asked.

She was so tempted to lie. To say gently that though she admired Mac, she felt nothing more than friendship for him. To assure the little girl with soothing words that her interests at Elk Valley Ranch lay only in her job and, in no way, involved taking Mac's time away with a new romance. Or possibly...love. The strong, solid kind Nicole had obviously enjoyed with Mac. The kind that might have the potential to take precedence over Nicole's memory.

But Dani had told too many lies already and Maddie's eyes were so clear—*so trusting*—that she couldn't bring herself to tell another. Not even to herself.

"Yes," she said softly. "I do."

"A lot?"

"Yes."

Maddie shot to her feet and scrubbed a hand over her red face. "Well, you can't. You can't like him. You were supposed to go back to New York."

"She can like Dad if she wants to," Nadine said, scooting quickly to Dani's side and threading her fingers through hers. "And she's staying here with us." She glanced up at Dani. "Aren't you?"

Dani licked her lips as they stared at her and scrambled for another honest answer. "I... I don't know for how long—"

"It's hot." Maddie dabbed at her cheeks with the hem of her shirt, rubbing hard at her eyes. "I want to go inside."

"We still have two flowers left to plant," Nadine said. "And it ain't that hot."

"It *is* hot."

Nadine shook her head and jumped to her feet, grumbling under her breath, "She can be such a sissy sometimes."

"I'm *not* a sissy." Maddie stamped her foot. "Stop saying that."

"I can say it if it's true—"

"Girls, please." Dani rose and brushed the dirt off her backside. "We were having such a good time and you were both doing a wonderful job. Why don't we go inside, have a glass of lemonade and cool off? Then, if it's not raining, we could come back out later and finish up?"

The girls remained silent, casting sour looks at each other.

"Maddie, does that sound like a good plan to you?" Dani asked.

Maddie dodged her eyes, her cheeks suspiciously wet, then nodded slowly. "I guess."

"Okay." Dani bent and grabbed one end of a large bag of potting soil. "Nadine, would you help me move these bags to the side of the stable? Tim and Cal might bring the horses in early if it storms and they'll need a clear path."

Nadine sighed, grabbed the other end and helped heft it out of the way. On the way back for another bag, she said, "Figures we'd end up inside again. That always happens." She scowled at her sister. "That's why Dad never lets us go hiking. He knows Maddie can't make it."

"That's enough, Nadine—"

"That's not true," Maddie shouted. "I could make it up the mountain."

Nadine scoffed. "Yeah, right."

"Nadine, I mean it." Dani leveled a stern look in her direction. "Let it go. We're going inside, putting our feet up and having a cool drink." Though, *dear God*, she needed something stronger than lemonade. "We could even watch a movie—*if*, you ask your sister very politely to accept your sincere apology for behaving rudely."

Nadine mulled this over for a minute, lips twisting and eyes rolling, then asked, "Maddie, will you please accept my apology for…" Brow creasing, she glanced at Dani in confusion before blurting, "Oh, yeah. For being rude and stuff."

Dani relaxed slightly. "Now, see—"

"I don't accept!" Maddie spun on her heel and ran off, her small figure darting across the field.

"Maddie, wait!"

"Aw, she'll be all right." Nadine shrugged then revealed a gap-toothed smile. "You want me to apologize again when we get inside? I can practice being more polite on you first so I can do it better next time."

Dani rubbed her forehead and groaned. *Good grief.* Could this morning possibly get any worse?

Mac took a hefty swig from a water bottle then handed it back to Jaxon as they stepped heavily along the winding mountain trail. "Thanks, buddy."

Jaxon smiled. "I packed plenty of everything, didn't I? Just like you taught me."

"Yep. You did a great job." Mac adjusted the thin hiking pack on his son's back. "Doesn't matter if you're walking one mile or eighty—always take your pack with you, yeah? You never know—"

"What might happen." Jaxon rolled his eyes and grinned, gesturing toward the bag hanging from Mac's shoulder. "Gah-lee, you've only told me that, like, a million times."

Mac bit back a laugh. "Getting on your nerves, am I?"

Jaxon harrumphed. "Well, sometimes, yeah."

He laughed. "Great. That means I'm being a good dad."

And for the first time in a long time, Mac actually believed it.

They began the long hike to the overlook this morning silently but, eventually, Mac had managed to bring Jaxon around to talking. First with jokes and anecdotes that entertained them with heavy breaths of laughter as they'd climbed the steep mountain, then with more solemn exchanges that prompted them to stray from the trail and prop up against an old oak while Jaxon shared his frustrations.

Jaxon had felt overlooked for a long time. That had been no surprise. But what had been a surprise was how mature and understanding his son had become.

Mac had reluctantly opened up about the ranch and the difficulties they faced—ones he'd hoped to protect his son from rather than share with him—but Jaxon seemed to already know how dire things had become.

He knew how hard Mac worked and understood his long hours even though he resented Mac at times for it.

Eventually, they'd reached an agreement of sorts, both making concessions to the other to help things run more smoothly in the future. It wouldn't be easy but it was a start, at least. And they'd had a damn good time together, too.

Mac smiled. A great time that he had Dani, in part, to thank for. Dani, whom he couldn't stop thinking about, though he'd been determined to keep things professional.

A low rumble of thunder rippled above them.

Mac glanced up at the thin trees towering over them as they neared the valley. The once-clear sky was now dark and the air around them had grown thicker during their descent from the overlook an hour ago. So charged and heavy, it almost crackled against the skin of his forearms. It seemed they'd timed their return to the ranch just right. He'd sensed an afternoon storm blowing in—they were almost like clockwork this time of year—and it looked like the trip to the creek with his girls would have to wait.

Mac smiled and picked up the pace. No worries. One advantage to business being slow was having full run of the lodge. The great room would be mostly empty, leaving plenty of space to build a blanket and pillow fort with the girls. They'd loved doing that last summer. He'd cut out paper stars with Maddie and helped Nadine string white lights, then collapsed inside the fort with them to read stories and do his best to answer a million questions. Questions on everything ranging from how many miles it was to a real star to how high a bullfrog could jump.

His smile widened. There was a stellar view of the valley from the great room, too. Dani would love it. Maybe she'd stick around and join them.

He stepped carefully over a chunk of loose rock and focused on the valley, which slowly came into view at the edge of the tree line. He'd keep it strictly business, of course. Just a friendly invitation to an employee to enjoy some well-deserved downtime. Under no circumstances would he kiss her again like he had last night. No matter how beautiful she was. Or how fantastic it'd felt.

They walked between the last set of trees then stepped onto the uneven path leading to the lodge. Mac's eyes strayed to the stretch of fence he and Dani had repaired last night. The memory of her soft lips clinging to his buzzed in his blood, sending a bolt of heat through his gut.

He grimaced. Strictly professional? *Yeah. Keep telling yourself that.*

"You think I could take Ms. Dani to the overlook one day?"

Mac refocused on Jaxon, nodding slowly. "I think she'd like that." Unlike Nicole, Dani loved the outdoors. He had yet to see her without dirt caked under her nails or her cheeks stained with sunburn. She wore both beautifully. "I'd think she'd love it, actually."

"Me, too," Jaxon said. "Think you might take her yourself sometime?" He hesitated for a moment. "Without me?"

He stifled a grin and studied Jaxon's hopeful expression. "What do you mean?"

"Well, she's nice. And fun. And…" Jaxon blushed. "And real pretty."

Mac lost the battle, laughter escaping him. "Oh, so you noticed that, huh?"

Jaxon glanced up at him, brows raised. "Yeah. Didn't you?"

"I expect I did."

Jaxon kicked a rock and tugged his pack higher on his back. "So I think you should ask her. You know, out on a date or something." His shoulders drew up and he laughed nervously. "I mean—it's just that... I'm thinking if I noticed and you noticed...then some other guy would probably notice, too. Then it'd be too late."

Mac's steps slowed. Discussing his love life with his son was uncomfortable enough without adding the thought of Dani with another man. He sure as hell didn't want to think about that. But dating an employee on his family's ranch with his children in tow? How in the world would that ever work out?

It'd been just him and the kids for years. If things did become serious with Dani, how would he go about finding a place for her in his life? In his family? In his heart?

And it wasn't just his heart on the line. His children had lost a lot, but if a potential relationship with Dani went bad there was still so much more that could be taken from them. Their sense of security after already having lost one mother. Their trust in others.

Was it even worth the risk to try?

As it was, his attention needed to be on his kids and trying to hold on to the ranch. Not Dani.

"Jaxon, you know I think a lot of Ms. Dani. But I'm not sure where things stand with us. And I won't jump into anything with her—or any woman—simply out of fear of what I might miss out on. If it's meant to be, it'll happen. At the right time." He sighed. "I know you miss Mom—I do, too—and we probably always will in some way or another. My dating or not dating won't change that. When I do decide to date again, it'll be with a woman I know will care about you and your sisters as much as I do."

Jaxon stared up at him, expression earnest. "Ms. Dani cares about us. Doesn't she?"

Mac hesitated. "She—"

"Mac!"

He swung around to find Cal racing up on horseback. The gelding skittered to a halt in front of Mac, dust billowing up beneath his hooves.

Cal glanced at Jaxon then the empty path behind them. "You didn't come across one of your girls on the way down, did you?"

Mac frowned. "No. They're with Dani."

"They *were*," Cal said. "Now one of 'em is missing."

Mac's heart skipped. "What? They were planting azaleas by the stable. They probably went inside to—"

"We already checked inside. Maddie's not in there. Dani said the girls had an argument and she ran off." Cal eased his mount around them then stopped, surveying the three hiking trails forking off in different directions. "I just finished checking the grounds with no sign of her. Tim and Dani split up and set off on the west trails a while ago, thinking she might've taken off up the mountain after you. Thought I'd head back up the east trail, just in case you missed her on your way back."

Lightning streaked above the valley, lighting up the dark sky.

Mac jerked into action, tugging Jaxon's pack from his shoulders and asking Cal, "Where's Nadine?"

"In the office with Ann."

"Which trail did Tim take?"

Cal pointed to the middle trail. "Dani took the one to Sugar Falls on foot. Didn't think she could navigate it on horseback. I'm going to take the overlook trail just to be thorough."

"Then I'll check behind Dani. Make sure we're covering every path."

"Want me to go with you, Dad?" Jaxon asked.

"No. Go on in and stay with Nadine." He hitched the extra pack over his shoulder and headed for the Sugar Falls trail. "Neither one of you are to step a toe outside of that lodge until I get back, yeah?"

"Yes, sir."

Mac walked briskly up the steep mountain trail, his heart thumping hard against his ribs as Cal's horse pounded up the overlook trail. Damn, he wished he had a horse, but trekking back to the stable and mounting up would cost him more time than it would just to head out on foot.

He hustled faster up the incline. The bags bounced against his back as he ascended and the trees grew thick again. His quads screamed with each step and his breath hitched, reminding him of just how far he and Jaxon had climbed this morning.

"Maddie!"

There was no answer. Just the rustling of branches as the breeze grew stronger.

Mac cringed. Why couldn't she and Nadine just stay put? Every time he turned around, they were gallivanting off somewhere without his permission. And he couldn't count the number of times he'd explicitly told them not to set off up the mountain without him.

Thunder bellowed through the trees and a gust of wind cut across the trail. Leaves scattered along the path and several heavy drops of rain pelted his forehead and jaw. Mac swallowed hard and shouted for Maddie again.

Listening for a response, he picked up the pace even more, his boots slipping on the loose dirt of the trail. It wasn't long before he'd covered over a mile, he guessed. The rain fell harder and his T-shirt clung wetly to his chest.

His throat tightened. The rain was heavier now. His view became obstructed by the haze of cascading water and the dirt path melted into mud beneath his feet. He had a hard time keeping his balance, which meant Maddie and Dani would, too.

Maddie had next to no climbing skills and Dani had no knowledge of the landscape. They wouldn't be able to see farther than a couple feet in front of them at most. And by then—

"Maddie!"

His mouth ran dry. He dragged his wet forearm over his drenched face, his steps stalling with helpless panic. Maddie was alone out here. Had been for some time in this storm. On this dangerous terrain. *His Maddie.* And Dani…

"—ac!"

He froze. The rush of wind and creaks of tree limbs quickly buried the faint voice in the distance.

Mac blinked hard against the rain pelting his eyelids and shouted, "Dani?"

"—er here!"

It *was* her. The cry spurred his burning legs forward, up the next swell of the trail then off the beaten path. He waited until he heard her voice again then followed it to the edge of the drop off and peered through the sheets of rain over the edge.

There she was, clinging to the sharp incline, her hands wrapped tightly around a thick protruding tree root and her feet scrambling for a foothold on slippery undergrowth as she looked down. It wasn't that far to the bottom, but it was steep enough to want to avoid a fall.

Small arms shifted around Dani's neck and a blond head lifted above her back. "Please don't drop me. It's muddy down there."

Maddie. Mac blew out a heavy sigh of relief. *Thank God.*

"Mud is the least of our worries," Dani said. "And there's no way I'd let go of you, Maddie. Just hold on to me and we'll be fine."

Mac dropped his packs to the ground and raised his voice above the onslaught of rain. "Dani."

She grunted then craned her neck, blinking rapidly up at him. "Oh, thank goodness." A relieved grin wavered across her face as she spat at the rain pouring over her lips. "I'm so sorry, Mac. I thought I knew the way back but I got lost when it started raining then Maddie fell. She's fine but I could really use a hand."

"Dad!" Maddie reached out toward him and edged further up Dani's back, causing her to flinch.

"Stay put, Maddie, and hold on to Dani."

Mac dropped to his knees beside a tree, grabbed the trunk with one arm for support then thrust the other over the edge. Dani released the tree root with one hand

and reached quickly for his, her wet fingers slipping over his skin and losing their grip.

Panic flickered across her face and she renewed her hold on the root.

"Easy, babe," he said over the pounding rain. "I'm not going anywhere. Go slow."

She did, successfully getting a grip on his hand, then his arm, and he wound his fingers around her elbow and pulled, dragging them up the incline. Dani wrapped her arms around his neck as he tugged them back onto the trail. They collapsed into a heap, Dani sprawling across his chest and Maddie splaying over Dani's back.

Their combined weight pressed Mac hard into the sludgy ground and his lungs strained to draw in air, but the sheer adoration on their faces as they stared down at him took all the pain away.

Mac wrapped his arms around them both then smiled up at Dani. "Get lost, did you? And here I thought it was men who were supposed to be bad with directions."

Chapter Six

"Just a little farther."

Mac tightened his hold on Maddie's hand then squeezed Dani's, leading them toward the cabin a few feet in front of them, barely visible through the heavy rain. Rather than letting up, the storm had grown fiercer after they'd peeled themselves off the muddy ground, checked Maddie for injuries then headed back toward the ranch. The rain had lashed at their faces and Maddie—though uninjured—was visibly exhausted. Deciding the cabin at Sweet Falls was closer, Mac had changed course to seek shelter and wait out the storm.

"We'll be inside soon," he continued. "Get you both cleaned up and comfortable."

Lightning flashed and bright white flooded the secluded lot for an instant before thunder rolled across the surrounding mountains. Maddie whimpered and Mac drew her tighter to his side. They trudged up the front steps of the cabin then Mac put his shoulder to the door, forcing the swollen wood open with a squeaky jerk.

"It looks worse than it is." He dropped the two backpacks he carried on the wood floor then pulled his cell phone from his soggy pocket and tossed it on the couch.

"Hmm, I've heard that somewhere before." Smiling, Dani closed the door behind them, her teeth bright against her muddy cheeks.

His heart kicked his ribs. God help him. Even drenched and muddied up, she was beautiful. "I haven't had a chance to stock it with supplies like I did yours but I cleaned it thoroughly and there's running water."

"Dad, my feet hurt."

Mac glanced down at Maddie. She clutched his wet shirt between clenched fists and her teeth chattered. The air outside had cooled considerably during their walk to the cabin and the goose bumps on her arms proved the chill had gotten to her.

"Time to get out of those wet clothes and into the shower," he said, lifting her into his arms and carrying her to the bathroom. "Dani, would you bring me those packs, please?"

He toed the lid of the toilet seat down then set Maddie on it and untied her shoes. Mud caked the laces, clinging to his fingers and plopping in clumps to the floor. He tugged them off and checked Maddie's feet for injuries, finding none. They were probably just sore from walking so far. A bit of discomfort as a result of disobeying just might do Maddie's stubbornness some good.

Dani placed the backpacks at his feet.

"Thanks." Mac unzipped Jaxon's pack, retrieved a dry T-shirt then frowned at Maddie. "You're lucky your brother did as I asked and packed for his hike. Otherwise you'd have nothing dry to change into."

Maddie looked down at her bare feet and curled her toes.

Mac shook his head. "I've told you a thousand times not to take off on those trails without me."

She bit her lip and tucked her chin tighter to her chest.

"Do you have any idea how many people you worried? We had no idea where you were or if you were hurt. Tim and Cal were still out looking for you when I called to tell them I found you."

"I'm sorry." Her shoulders jerked on a smothered sob and she raised her head, tears in her eyes. Chin wobbling, she looked over his shoulder. "I'm really sorry, Ms. Dani. I didn't mean to make anyone worry."

"I know you didn't," Dani said softly.

Mac sighed. The gentle tone of Dani's voice eased some of the tension from his body as it drifted over him. Maddie relaxed, too. Her shoulders lowered and she wiped away a tear that rolled down her cheek.

"Are you sure you're okay?" Dani continued. "You don't hurt anywhere else besides your feet?"

"No ma'am," Maddie whispered, studying her toes again. "I'm okay."

Mac glanced at Dani. "What about you? You didn't twist an ankle climbing down that embankment, did you?"

"No, I'm good. Just a few cuts on my hands." She gestured toward the sink. "I'd like to clean them and wash this mud off my face before Maddie jumps in the shower, if you don't mind?"

"Of course," he said. "Check my pack. There's a first-aid kit in there with some antibiotic ointment. Wouldn't hurt to use some of that."

She thanked him, retrieved the ointment from the bag then turned on the faucet. He watched her reflection in the mirror above the sink, noticing her flinch and grimace when the water hit her hands.

"It wasn't just you that could've been hurt, Maddie." Mac squatted in front of her and nudged her chin up with a knuckle. "You put Ms. Dani in danger, too. She's never hiked these trails before. Doesn't know the land like we do. She could've broken a leg climbing down to get you. Could've—"

"Mac." Dani paused in the act of patting her face dry. Her eyes drifted to Maddie, softening as they settled on his daughter. "We're both fine. That's what matters. And it's my fault, too. I should have been more vigilant."

He studied her face. There was no mistaking the intensity of concern in her expression and voice. It was the same demeanor she'd had when she'd spoken to him about Jaxon. Tender and caring. So much so that it lightened the heavy weight in his chest.

"I *am* sorry, Dad. And I really didn't want to worry anyone."

"Then why'd you do it?"

Maddie wrapped her small hands around his forearms. "I just wanted to show you that I could climb the mountain, too. That I could be as strong as Jaxon."

"Jaxon is three years older than you," Mac said. "And much bigger, too. It stands to reason that he might be physically stronger than you. You're strong in your own way. And in three years, who knows? You might be stronger than he was at that age."

"I know but he and Nadine are good at hiking and fishing. I tried to make it up the mountain but I couldn't do it. And I can't fish good because the worms scare me sometimes. I can't do half the stuff they can. And I thought you might…"

Mac softened his voice. "Tell me, Maddie."

She hesitated, then whispered, "That you might love Jaxon and Nadine more than me because…"

"Because they can do those things?" Mac prompted.

She nodded. "And I thought that if I showed you I could do it, you'd—"

Her voice broke. Fresh tears streamed down her cheeks then pooled in the corners of her mouth.

The warmth rising in Mac's chest intensified to a strong burn, blurring his vision. How in the hell could he have been so blind to his children's needs? He'd been so damned busy trying to hold on to the ranch that he'd made excuses to justify ignoring his children. First Jaxon, now Maddie.

And the thought of her feeling as though she didn't measure up for him…

As though he wasn't proud of her or didn't love her…

He shook his head and cupped her face in his hands. "Maddie, don't you know I love you just the way you are?" The surprise in her eyes sent a fresh wave of guilt through him. "That there's nothing in this world you could ever do—or not do—that would make me love you any less?"

She remained silent for a moment, then sniffed. "Really?"

"Really."

"But what if…" Her chest lifted on a big breath and she looked at Dani, cheeks flushing.

Dani slipped the ointment into the backpack then backed toward the door. "I'll wait outside," she said softly, closing the door behind her.

Mac waited as Maddie took a few breaths and fiddled with the muddy buttons on her shirt. "What is it? You can talk to me about anything."

"Ms. Dani's good at those things, too. Not like me." She frowned. "You said I'm a lot like Mama, right?"

"Yeah. Very much so."

Maddie stared up at him. "You said she liked marshmallows and the stars. But she didn't like to go hiking."

Mac smiled. "She did on occasion but it wasn't her favorite thing to do. And there was absolutely nothing wrong with that. I loved your mother just the way she was."

"Will you always?" she pressed.

"Your mother will always be in my heart, Maddie."

"And me, too?"

"Of course."

"But what happens if you love someone else?" Her voice shook, the words rushed.

He held his breath. "Are you talking about Ms. Dani?"

Maddie nodded slowly. "Ms. Dani said she liked you. A lot. I asked her this morning and that's what she told me. Do you like her, too?" She gripped his arms tighter. "Because me and Ms. Dani can't both fit in your heart, can we?"

Mac sat back on his heels, an odd mixture of emotions engulfing him. Pleasure at the notion that Dani might think of him as much as he thought of her. And sadness that Maddie would ever need to weigh such heavy concerns in her young mind.

Lord, he wished he knew how to answer her. Which words to use. Nicole had always been the better parent. If she were here, she would know exactly the right thing to say.

Actually…she already had.

He smiled. "Do you know what your mama said right after you and your sister were born?"

Maddie shook her head.

"My arms runneth over." He laughed. "The nurse had put you in one of her arms and Nadine in the other and she could barely hold on to the two of you because y'all were wiggling so much. And Jaxon," he rubbed his palm over his wet jeans. "Jaxon was standing by the door. He was tiny then—three years old—and he looked like he felt out of place. Like maybe, since your mama had her arms full with you and Nadine, there wasn't room for him anymore."

He waited, watching as Maddie frowned, considering this.

"You know what your mama did?" Maddie's green eyes widened up at him in question. "She told him to climb up on the bed, stretch out across her middle and put his head on her chest between the two of you. That his little sisters needed him and that spot would always be just for him."

Maddie blinked, a small smile appearing.

"Hearts grow, Maddie. As big as we need them to. You, Nadine, Jaxon—and your mama—all have your own special place in my heart. No matter who I end up caring for, that will never change."

Her smile widened, lighting her eyes and flushing her cheeks. She threw her arms around his neck and squeezed.

Mac held Maddie close and hugged her back, remembering how great it'd felt earlier being pressed into that mud by both Maddie and Dani. How comforting their weight had been over his chest and how perfectly they'd fit into his arms. How one smile from Dani had given him a glimpse of sunlight in the midst of all that rain.

And he no longer questioned if it was possible to find a place in his life—or heart—for Dani. Because he had a feeling she was already there.

"I'M SORRY FOR lying to you, Mac. Sorry for pretending to be someone else and trying to take your land. Sorry for not telling you the truth sooner. And sorry for…"

Dani froze, her whispered words sticking in her throat. Just say it. *Say it.*

"For losing both your horse and daughter in less than twenty-four hours."

Oh, God. It sounded even more ridiculous spoken out loud than it had when she'd recited it in her head. She slumped over the bathroom sink, pressed her forehead to the steamed-up mirror and rolled it from side to side.

This was quite possibly the worst moment of her life.

No. Scratch that. The worst moment had been sliding down the side of a mountain with Maddie, unsure of whether or not she could actually maintain her hold on the little girl. *That* had been terrifying.

"Get it together, Dani." She blew out a breath. "And stop talking to yourself."

She straightened then dug around in Mac's backpack. He'd left the bathroom with a freshly showered Maddie just a half hour earlier, offering Dani the use of the shower, too, and telling her she was welcome to wear the clean T-shirt and jeans in his bag while hers dried out, if she liked.

Soaked to the skin, Dani had eagerly accepted. The

hot shower and her now mud-free hair made her feel tons better. On the outside, at least. If only she could feel as renewed on the inside.

She found the jeans and put them on, rolling the waistband over twice, then took out the T-shirt. Her hands stilled. Of course, there was another option. She could quit quietly, leave Mac and the children and drive back to New York. Let things at Elk Valley Ranch play out naturally. Mac had made it clear he wasn't selling so there was no longer any reason for her to stay. Except for the way he made her feel...

Her throat tightened. Exciting and passionate. As though she was strong and whole. As though she fit, right here in Elk Valley. And the thought of going back to New York—

No. Leaving without telling Mac the truth wasn't a viable option. It was a coward's way out. The only way she could feel remotely good about herself again would be to come clean with Mac and beg for his forgiveness.

Then, she'd have to hope he could manage not to hate her.

Oh, please, please don't hate me. Fingers shaking, she closed her eyes and tugged the shirt over her head. Mac was a fair man. One of many virtues he possessed that she admired.

The collar caught on her nose. He'd understand. He—

She stilled, breathing through the soft cotton. *Oh, he smelled so good.* Like man. Pine. Soap.

Her eyes lifted in tandem with another inhale and focused on her wet bra, dangling over the top of the shower stall. The image made her acutely aware of the fabric of Mac's shirt as it slid over her bare skin and settled against her belly.

Good grief, she had to get out of here and get some fresh air. Dani snatched up a washcloth, the only dry towel left, then left the bathroom. The door to the bedroom where Mac had taken Maddie was still closed. She slipped quietly to the back of the cabin then outside onto the wooden deck.

The rain had stopped but a mist hovered on the cool air and the sound of rushing water echoed against the thick foliage nestled around the cabin. Squeezing her wet hair with the small towel, she rounded the corner to the other side of the cabin and looked down.

Clear water flowed freely over smooth stones down a wide creek, then cascaded into a waterfall. The swift current kicked up a soft breeze, which rustled the thick green leaves on bushes and caused thin, low-lying tree limbs to dance.

Her hand stilled against her hair. "Beautiful."

"Sugar Falls."

Startled, she glanced over her shoulder to find Mac standing on the deck. He'd discarded his wet shirt and the dark blond hair on his wide muscular chest arrowed down to his lean hips where his soggy jeans clung to the thick muscles of his thighs.

Her breath caught in her throat and she forced herself to refocus on his face.

His green eyes darkened as they traveled slowly from her head down to her toes. He smiled and the grooves on either side of his mouth deepened, accentuating his strong stubble-lined jaw. "That outfit damned sure looks better on you than it does me."

Heat swirled in her belly and her limbs grew heavy.

"Here." He walked over and took the washcloth from her hand, the blunt tips of his fingers smoothing across her knuckles. "Let me."

His big palms brushed the sides of her neck as he gathered her wet hair in his hands and began drying it gently with the towel. The chorus of crickets and frogs chirping almost in rhythm with the current and his slow caressing movements lulled her eyes closed.

She pried them back open and tried to focus on a large log floating downstream. "Where's Maddie?"

"Asleep in the bedroom. Once she got still, she drifted off. I couldn't bring myself to wake her." He stepped closer, his hard chest grazing her back as he began kneading the hair at her nape. "Thought I'd let her take a nap before we head back. That okay with you?"

Her head dropped forward and her eyes slid shut again. "Mmm hmm."

He chuckled, the low sound vibrating against her.

Face flaming, she tucked her chin tighter to her chest. "I'm so sorry about Maddie. I really thought she'd gone back inside and it wasn't until Nadine and I went to the lodge that I realized she'd left. I should've been paying more attention to—"

"You have nothing to apologize for." He leaned closer, his voice deep by her ear. "She and Nadine are known to slip off and they've gotten away from me more than once. She knew better. Besides, I should be the one thanking you for going after her."

Dani glanced at the cuts on her hands and shuddered. "We were lucky you came along when you did."

"Maybe," he said softly. "But whether I came along

or not, you would've made it back up that mountain okay. You're too strong and determined not to."

She smiled. "You think?"

"I know." His hands paused in her hair. "You really care about Maddie, don't you? And Nadine and Jaxon?"

"Yes." Thinking of Jaxon's headstrong attitude, Nadine's rambunctious nature and Maddie's tender heart made something flutter in her chest. "It'd be impossible not to. They're amazing children."

They grew silent, watching the water flow and listening to the sounds of the forest.

"My parents used to bring us here when we were kids." Mac continued towel-drying her hair, pausing at her temples and massaging the delicate skin. "There's a fishing hole up the creek a ways. Nate loved it. He used to catch a ton of trout."

"Nate's your brother?"

"Yeah."

She tipped her head back toward his magic touch, leaning into him, and tried not to slur her words. "Older or younger?"

"Younger."

His fingers drifted down to rub her neck and she bit back a groan, searching for something coherent to say. "How much younger?"

Mac moved closer. His thick thighs nudged the back of hers. "Not by much." There was a smile in his voice. "Why? You're not more interested in him than me, are you?"

She twisted, narrowing her eyes up at him. "Who said I'm interested in you?"

"Maddie. I believe you said you liked me." He grinned. "A lot."

She turned back to the creek, hiding a smile. "Do you see your brother often?"

He laughed, tossing the washcloth onto the rail then moving his palms to her shoulders. "Not a very smooth attempt at changing the subject, but I'll bite." His laughter trailed off. "No, I don't see Nate often. He rides bulls. Stays on the rodeo circuit. Thanksgiving and Christmas are usually the only times of year I can count on seeing him."

Dani stilled. She and Scott had always been close and these past weeks at Elk Valley had been the longest she'd gone without seeing him. It was difficult to imagine going almost a year without spending time with her brother.

"You must miss him," she said.

Mac murmured an assent.

"And your parents?" She hesitated. "What happened to them?"

He was silent for a moment. "My mom died of a heart attack years ago. It was a shock for all of us but especially my dad." His voice grew tight. "I don't think he ever got over it. He worked himself into the ground. A year afterward, he was gone, too."

Her vision blurred. Mac had not only lost his wife but he'd lost his parents, as well. Rarely saw his brother. No wonder he was so fiercely protective of his home.

She reached up, capturing his wrists with her hands and squeezing. "I'm sorry, Mac. That must have been awful for you."

He went back to massaging her shoulders, voice heavy. "They were good people."

Dani turned to face him. His smile had dimmed and his eyes were shadowed.

"I know," she said. "They had to be to raise a man like you."

The corner of his mouth lifted. "A man like me?"

She nodded. "Honest, loyal and fair." Her stomach flipped. All things she wished she were better at. "And you're a great father, Mac. What you have with Jaxon and Nadine and Maddie…"

The tender look in his eyes made her skin tingle.

"I wish I had that," Dani whispered. "I wish my father knew me like you know Maddie. That he—"

…*Don't you know I love you just the way you are?*

She shook her head, unable to get Mac's words out of her mind. The gentle tone and firm assurance. The very thing she'd yearned to hear from her father for so long.

"You asked me why I left New York and it was true that I needed a change. But I didn't tell you the whole truth." She swallowed hard. "I came because I needed to prove something to my father. I guess I was being a lot like Maddie, trying to show him I was strong and could do things on my own. I thought if I could come here and succeed that he'd approve of me. Accept me. That when I went back to New York, maybe I'd feel like I finally fit in."

Mac stared down at her, eyes roving over her face.

"But honestly, I'm starting to not want to go back," she continued. "Back there I stick out." She laughed, the sound dry and humorless even to her own ears. "And not in a good way. But I feel different here. *You* make me feel different." She hesitated, searching for the right way to say it. "Here, I feel like I fit. I feel like you understand me." Her cheeks burned, her simple words sounding more gauche than ever. "Like you get me."

He drifted a cool finger across her flaming cheekbone. "You get me, too." His big hand wrapped around hers then lifted it to his chest, pressing her palm tight to his skin, the heavy throb of his heart beating against her fingertips. "Right here."

Something shifted in her chest, making her legs weak. She opened her mouth and tried to speak. *Just say it. Tell him everything. You have to tell him.*

"I haven't been completely honest with you, either," he said.

She froze, eyes meeting his as he moved closer.

"I lied when I told you I didn't intend to kiss you last night." He cupped her face, tilting her chin up to his. "It's all I've thought about for two weeks. What it'd feel like to hold you. To touch you. Taste you." His expression darkened as he studied her. "I don't want to keep things professional. I want to make them personal. And I meant to kiss you last night." He lowered his head. "Just like I mean to now."

He covered her mouth with his, parting her lips with his tongue and sweeping inside. He filled her senses, his male scent surrounding her, his intoxicating taste enveloping her tongue and his touch sending tingles over her skin. Her entire body lit up on the inside.

Dani wrapped her arms around him and kissed him back, her hands kneading over his bare shoulders, his hair-roughened chest and then his chiseled abs. He groaned and gripped her hips, lifting his mouth from hers and dragging in air.

She pressed closer and threaded her fingers through the thick hair above his nape. "More."

His eyes darted over her. To her hips. Her chest. Legs then mouth. As though he couldn't decide where to focus. "More?"

At her nod, he lifted her against him then walked backward and leaned against the cabin wall. Easing a thigh between hers, he kissed her again, his lips leaving hers to travel down her neck. His tongue teased a tender spot below her ear, shooting delicious bolts of sensation through her body. She stifled a cry of pleasure and dropped her head back, lifting her chest toward his roving mouth.

He complied, stringing open-mouthed kisses along her collarbones and sliding his hands beneath her shirt. His palms cupped her bare breasts, his calloused thumbs brushing gently across the sensitive peaks. They both moaned and he dropped his forehead against hers, their heavy breaths mingling.

The sound of rushing water and rustling leaves were barely discernible over the heavy pounding of her heart. His broad hands still moved slowly under her shirt, caressing her breasts and making her sag against him.

Dani smoothed her fingertip over his bottom lip and smiled, feeling like a giddy teenager again. "Are we really necking in the woods, right now?"

"Yeah." He grinned and smoothed his hands over her back. "And it feels…"

The raspy note in his voice made her meet his passion-filled eyes.

"Fan—"

"—tastic."

They spoke at the same time then burst out laughing. Maybe it was the sexy glint in his eyes. Or that endearing dimple in his chin. Whatever it was, Dani found herself tugging his mouth back to hers for a deeper kiss.

Mac hugged her closer and spun them around. He pressed her to the wall just as his left boot crashed through a rotten wood plank in the deck. "What the hell—"

"Oh, no!" She scrambled for a grip on his biceps as he struggled to maintain his balance.

He braced himself with a hand on the cabin wall then jerked his boot free of the hole, muttering a string of curses under his breath.

"Are you okay?" she asked.

He nodded, leaning back to peer around the corner of the cabin.

She froze and listened with him for any sounds of movement. Thankfully, there were none. Maddie was still asleep inside.

Dani cleared her throat nervously then smiled up at Mac.

He grinned as he smoothed her shirt down over her jeans. "Guess this isn't the safest place to fool around."

She laughed. "Then where would you suggest?"

He tucked a wet strand of her hair behind her ear then traced his fingertip down her neck—the same path he'd kissed. "The overlook, next Friday night." His smile faded as he glanced down at the ragged hole in the deck. "Figure I should take the kids camping at least one more time before this place completely falls apart."

Dani froze, the reminder of Mac's circumstances sending a chill—and a fresh wave of guilt—through her. She was digging this hole of deceit so deep she may never be able to climb out. But telling the truth meant possibly losing him altogether.

"Hey." He tapped her chin and grinned. "There'll be a campfire, stars and more kisses, guaranteed. It'll be fun. I promise."

Dani's head screamed it was a bad idea. That she should politely decline, tell Mac the truth now and accept the consequences, whatever they ended up being.

But her heart said otherwise.

"I'd love to."

Chapter Seven

Mac had a routine for packing before a hike. A fast, efficient method that ensured he was always well-prepared for a night of camping.

It took his kids two minutes to shoot it all to hell.

"No, Maddie." Mac tugged another pile of clothes from her bag. "You're not taking eight sundresses for one night of camping."

"I have to take them," she said, plopping onto the grass beside her bag. She shielded her eyes against the afternoon sun and looked up at him. "I need them."

"What for?"

"For after we swim in the creek. I'll need something dry to put on."

"That's why we picked out two pairs of shorts and two shirts," Mac said. "You'll have one dry outfit to wear when you get out and the wet set will be dry by morning for when we start back."

"But it'll be dirty—"

"*We'll* be dirty, Maddie." He took a long, calming breath. "That's part of camping."

"I don't like that part." She frowned. "And I want to take my dresses."

Good Lord. At this rate, it'd be sundown before they even started.

Mac smothered a groan then stared past her toward the hiking trail. It was four o'clock. They were supposed to have left for the overlook an hour ago but he'd underestimated the challenges of helping three children pack for one night outdoors. And the effect one thin piece of paper could have on him.

"We got the snacks, Dad."

Grass rustled at Mac's back and he glanced over his shoulder. Jaxon and Nadine walked across the field, their backpacks fully packed and settled on their backs. He breathed a sigh of relief.

Finally, a break—

"Wait." Mac held up a hand, watching as they drew to an abrupt halt, overstuffed grocery bags clutched in each of their hands and swinging against their legs. "What's in those?"

"Pork skins." Jaxon smiled and lifted one of the bags. "And chips and salsa and—"

"Soda, cheese dip and video games," Nadine added.

"Nope." Mac shook his head, walked over and tugged at the bags. "No, no, no. Y'all are going to put all of this right back where you got it from. I don't want you carrying more than—at most—ten percent of your body weight. Besides, the purpose of this trip is to spend time together. You won't have time for video games and I've already packed all the food we need."

Jaxon scowled. "But, Dad—"

"What food did you pack?" Nadine asked, tugging back at the bags. "Cuz I don't like that stinky chili stuff you usually bring."

"Chili?" Maddie stuck out her tongue. "Yuck."

Mac gritted his teeth. "Nadine, let go of the bag."

She pulled harder. "But—"

"Everything okay?" Smiling, Dani walked up, eyeing his grocery bag tug-of-war with Nadine.

The sun hit her just right, shining through her hair, highlighting her pink cheeks and bouncing off her white T-shirt where it clung to her sexy curves.

Mac's heart skipped a beat. The remembered feel of her in his arms made his hands itch to reach for her again.

Jaxon shrugged. "Dad said we can't take the chips and salsa."

"Or the soda," Nadine said, cutting her eyes up at Mac.

"Dad?" Maddie asked.

He turned, watching as she peered into her backpack. "What is it, Maddie?"

"I forgot my sleeping bag."

Jaxon scoffed.

Mac sighed. "I think we just need to start over and repack your bag."

"Start over?" Maddie asked. "But that'll take forever."

Mac closed his eyes and rubbed his temples. "I know."

"Mac?" Dani's hand, supportive and soft, curled around his. "Are you all right?"

He opened his eyes and drudged up a smile. "Yeah. Why?"

She put her back to the kids and whispered, "You seem upset about more than just backpacks. And you've been like this all week."

He looked down and dragged his boot over the

grass, watching the blades slowly spring back up. The past few days had been tough. He hadn't kissed Dani since the storm and he was unsettled by the intensity of feelings she aroused in him. That damned broken deck at Sugar Falls had been bugging him all week and he still hadn't had a chance to fix it yet, despite another slow bout of business. Cal, Tim and Dani had worked their tails off on the grounds every day but he'd begun to fear that no amount of new business could save the ranch.

To top it all off, the worst of his worries had materialized this morning, forcing him to dwell on facts he could no longer ignore. His mouth twisted. Figured it'd happen on the one day he'd set aside to spend time with Dani and the kids.

"I'm fine." He weaved his fingers through hers. "Just got a lot on my mind."

"Then you picked the perfect day for this camping trip," she said. "Because we're going to have fun, just like you said." She smiled. "No matter what."

Her teasing coaxed a grin from him. "Is that right?"

"Yes. I don't know about you, but I've been looking forward to this all week and it'll do us all some good." She nudged him toward the stable. "Now, why don't you check the grounds one last time before we leave? While you do that, Nadine and Jaxon will put that food back in the kitchen and I'll help Maddie repack her bag. Then, we'll take off."

"As simple as all that, huh?"

"Yes," she said, pushing him harder. "Now go, then meet us back here in ten minutes."

He laughed. "Yes, ma'am."

Strolling across the grounds, Mac stared up at the

mountain peaks, taking deep breaths and flexing his hands. He made his way to the stable where Cal was mucking stalls.

"Thought y'all had already set out," Cal said, dumping a shovel full of waste into the wheelbarrow.

"We're about to. Just looking things over before we leave." Mac grabbed a bag of clean shavings and moved it closer to the stall. "Where's Tim?"

"Took the horses on the trail. No guests riding today but he figured the horses could use the exercise."

Mac nodded. "Were you the one that brought in the mail this morning?"

Cal glanced up then went back to sifting through shavings again. "I always do."

"Then I guess you saw it?"

Cal didn't answer, just kept scraping his shovel across the stall floor.

"The envelope from the bank," Mac said. "The one marked final notice?"

Cal straightened and propped an arm on his shovel. "Yeah. I saw it." He dragged his arm over his sweaty forehead. "Didn't think it was my place to mention it."

"Why? It concerns you." Mac looked out the open door of the stable, across the green field to where Dani and the kids were repacking Maddie's bag on the grass. "If you have any questions, this is a good time to ask."

Cal remained silent.

"I'm not budging 'til I'm forced out. But you know when the time comes, I'll take care of you and Tim, right?" Mac looked at Cal. "Landon Eason's got a lot of land just up the road and he's mentioned on more than one occasion that he could use some extra help.

I'll put in a good word for you both and you're guaranteed the job if you want it."

Cal knuckled his hat higher on his head. "Is that where you'll go? Eason's spread?"

Mac shook his head, gut roiling. "I can't stay in Elk Valley knowing I'll never own this ranch again. It'd be too hard being that close and that far away at the same time."

"So what'll you do?"

Mac's shoulders slumped, his fears growing so heavy they almost suffocated him. "Start over somewhere else." He refocused on Maddie as she stood up in the field and tugged her backpack on her shoulders. "That's all I can do."

Two hours later, Mac, Dani and the kids cleared the final swell of the trail leading to the overlook. The rocky dirt path ended and an open stretch of grass led to a wooden fence at the edge of the mountain. Sunlight cast gold and rosy undertones through the misty haze covering the mountain peaks in the distance.

"I did it," Maddie shouted, hugging Mac's leg.

"You sure did, baby." Mac ruffled her blond hair then laughed as she and Nadine chased each other in circles, squealing with excitement, their packs bouncing on their backs.

"See. Told you we needed this." Dani, slightly out of breath from the hike, leaned on the top rail of the fence. "Wow. I didn't think it could more beautiful than Sugar Falls." She whistled low, her face flushed a pretty pink and excitement in her dark eyes. "This is unbelievable, Mac."

Unbelievable. He reached out and trailed his knuckles down her soft cheek. That was the perfect word for his current circumstances. For life giving him Dani the same time it took this land from him. He couldn't imagine a more ironic high and low.

What would she do when he lost this place? Last week, she said she didn't want to leave Elk Valley and return to New York. That she felt like she fit... with him. And he felt the same. Her pull on him was powerful.

His chest tightened. But would she be willing to pack up and move in the same direction as him? Start all over again and look for a new job with a man and three children when this connection between them was still so new and uncertain?

"Look, girls." Dani tipped her head back and pointed toward the blue sky. "Aren't they beautiful?"

Two large birds drifted high on the breeze, wings spread. Nadine and Maddie skipped to Dani's side and looked up.

"Are those eagles, Dad?" Nadine asked.

Mac grinned. "'Fraid not. Those are vultures."

"Yep," Jaxon said, jumping onto a log and walking it, arms spread. "The kind that eat roadkill. They're probably looking for a rotten opossum or skunk."

"Ew." Nadine and Maddie made retching noises.

Dani shrugged then smiled. "Well, a girl can dream, can't she? We'll just pretend they're eagles."

Mac laughed and shifted closer, taking her hand in his and pressing his arm against hers. Her smooth skin felt like silk, making him long to kiss her again. To see if she tasted as sweet as he remembered.

"Dad." Maddie yanked at his backpack. "It's hot. Can we go to the creek now?"

"Don't see why not." Mac tugged Dani's hand and

started for the trail leading down to the creek. "We only have a couple hours of daylight left though, so we'll need to set up the tents first."

"Girls in one and boys in the other." Maddie skipped ahead, asking over her shoulder, "Right, Dad?"

Mac smiled ruefully, squeezing Dani's hand. "Unfortunately."

"What?" Maddie asked.

Dani stifled a laugh with her free hand.

"Nothing, Maddie," Mac said.

They set up camp in a flat area closest to the creek. Tall trees offered shade but the immediate area around the tents was open, allowing for an unimpeded view of the sky. It'd been a clear day and should be a clear night with a fantastic view. Just like Mac had hoped.

After securing the tents, unpacking necessities for the night and settling two disagreements between the kids, Mac was ready to wade through the creek.

The current was swift and the water looked inviting.

"I want to build a fort this time," Jaxon said, plopping onto a big rock and tugging off his boots.

"Me, too." Nadine stood on one foot and pulled at the sock on the other.

Mac smiled, walked to the edge and stuck his hand beneath the swift current. Despite the hot weather, the water was cool. Almost too cool.

"It's still kinda col—"

Water smacked him in the face, stinging his eyes and dripping off his chin. He sucked in a strong breath at the icy shock, dragged a hand over his face then looked to his left.

Dani and Maddie were crouched on a smooth rock

at the edge of the water. They grinned at each other, then at him.

"Hmm," Dani said, rubbing her chin. "I think we should go in slow, Maddie. It looks like the water might be cold."

Mac laughed. "You rotten rascals." He stood slowly then headed toward them. "Cold, huh? I'll show you cold."

Maddie squealed and took off, ducking behind her brother. Dani started after her but Mac managed to grab the waistband of her jeans.

"Oh no, you don't."

He picked her up, swinging her high up against his chest, then stomped into the creek, splashing cold water up his legs.

"No, Mac, please." Dani laughed, wrapped her arms around his neck and tried climbing further up his chest. "I'm sorry. It was an accident."

Mac waded deeper. "Accident, my foot."

The kids cheered at his back, egging him on.

"Get her, Dad," Jaxon shouted, laughing.

When the water reached his hips, Mac sat on his butt and dropped backward, dunking himself and Dani under the swift current. He sat up and squeezed Dani tight to his middle as she sputtered and laughed through the water streaming down her face.

"You don't play fair," she gasped.

Mac grinned, the cold water numbing his legs. "You started it."

"I splashed you. I didn't dunk you."

"Maybe you should have." Mac's chest swelled as she hugged him close and shivered, still laughing. "Come on." He held on to her with one arm and shoved to his feet with his other. "Time to get you out and dried off."

After leaving the creek, they squeezed their wet clothes dry as best they could then settled on a big rock overlooking the creek while the kids splashed and played. The sun had dipped low in the sky but the smooth stone beneath them was warm to the touch.

"Come here." Mac held out his hand to Dani and she took it, nudging his knees apart and sitting between them with her back resting against his chest.

"The sun feels so good." She tipped her head back against his shoulder, eyes closed, and smiled. "My cushion is pretty comfortable, too."

Mac laughed and wrapped his arms around her soft middle. "I aim to please."

Her long lashes lifted and her blue eyes looked up at him, full of adoration. "You have. Thank you for inviting me. It's beautiful here."

He studied the curve of her mouth and the new batch of freckles sprinkled across her nose then lifted a wet wave of her hair and wound it loosely around his finger. Touching his lips to it, he breathed in the sweet scent of her mingling with the creek water, his heart damn near breaking.

"I'm going to lose this place, Dani."

She stiffened against him.

"A final notice came today," he said. "I knew it was inevitable. Knew it was coming. But I guess holding that paper in my hand made it real. So real that I can't see what I used to." His throat tightened and he looked at Jaxon and the girls stepping gingerly through the creek, gathering stones and stacking them. "I used to imagine at least one of the kids getting married in the valley someday like I did. I could see it so clearly. Could see them walking across that green field to take their vows, knowing they'd always have a home here. I used to be able to imagine one, if not all, of them taking over the ranch when I could no longer physically manage it." A strained laugh escaped him. "I could see them patting my old, worn-out shoulder and assuring me they knew what they were doing. Could see this land flourishing under their hands." He swallowed hard. "But the reality is, this could be the last time my kids walk that path and wade through that creek, knowing they're home."

Dani's back lifted against him on a shaky breath and he looked down at her. Tears spilled over her lashes and rolled down her face.

He brushed his thumb over her wet cheek, chest aching. "What would you do, Dani, if you had to start over? Where would you go?"

She didn't speak at first. Just turned her head and watched the kids stack stones for several minutes. Then she took his hand in hers and kissed his palm.

"I'm already starting over," she whispered. "Here. With you."

DANI BROKE A long narrow stick in half over her knee then handed one half to Jaxon. "There. Now everyone has a stick, right?"

Nadine and Maddie, seated on the ground by their brother, nodded.

"Great." Dani tossed the remaining half of the stick into the campfire. The flames flickered then crackled, sending a spray of red ash toward the night sky. "Let's get started."

She returned to her seat beside Mac and grabbed the bag of marshmallows on the blanket.

"Don't you need one?" Mac asked.

She glanced up as she opened the bag and grinned. "Nope. Someone has to have their hands free for this to work."

His lips quirked. "For what to work?"

"You'll see." She handed him a marshmallow, motioning for him to put it on the end of his stick. "Just roast your marshmallow and be patient."

The lip quirk morphed into a full-blown smile. "Yes, ma'am."

Satisfied, Dani nodded and passed the marshmallow bag around to the kids. It was so good to see Mac smile again. He'd grown quiet after their conversation by the creek and after they'd helped the children dry off and returned to camp, he'd left to collect firewood.

He was gone so long, she'd begun to worry, but he'd eventually returned with an armful of logs. After building the campfire, she'd helped him heat up five servings of chili—much to the kids' dismay—then announced it was time for dessert.

"Can I put two marshmallows on my stick?" Maddie asked, digging around in the bag again.

"Why don't we just start with one for now?" Dani tugged her backpack closer and retrieved two containers. "That's all you need for the dessert I have planned. Then, once you've tried it, you can add another if you'd like."

"Okay." Maddie smiled and stuck her marshmallow back over the flames.

Nadine and Jaxon followed suit and they waited patiently for the marshmallows to roast.

Dani watched the sparks drifting up on the night air and tipped her head back, watching as they ascended. The treetops swayed gently with the breeze, and stars glistened like diamonds on black velvet above them.

"It's a beautiful night," Dani said, glancing at Mac.

He looked up briefly, nodded then returned his attention to the campfire.

She frowned, wanting so much to wrap her arms around him. His words by the creek had been so full of pain and regrets that she knew they would overshadow any fun he managed to have tonight. And he deserved to enjoy time with his children. He deserved to be happy.

"Mine's ready," Jaxon said, removing his marshmallow from the flames.

"Bring it over here, please." Dani pried the lids off the two containers then grabbed a graham crackers and a piece of chocolate.

"S'mores." Jaxon smiled. "We haven't had those in a long time, Dad."

"What's a moor?" Nadine asked.

"S'mores." Dani frowned. "You've never had one before?"

"Not the girls," Mac said. "They've only been camping twice and Nicole…" He shrugged then looked away.

"Mom just liked the marshmallows," Jaxon said. "Not the other stuff."

"Yeah," Maddie said. "We just roast the marshmallows. Dad said Mama used to help us make them at the lodge."

"Well, it'll still be a roasted marshmallow." Dani smiled. "Just think of it as…an enhanced roasted marshmallow."

Jaxon lowered his stick, placing the marshmallow on the chocolate-laden cracker Dani held out. "I'll take one."

"Good." Dani grabbed another cracker. "I'll squish it together and you pull the stick out."

He did so and the girls stood on their tiptoes, watching as Jaxon brought the gooey concoction to his mouth and took a big bite.

"Is it good?" Nadine asked.

Jaxon grinned, melted marshmallow stringing from his lips and down his chin. "Itf weally gwood."

The girls pulled their sticks from the fire and stuck them out toward Dani, saying simultaneously, "I want one."

"Remember your manners, girls," Mac admonished.

Maddie blushed.

Nadine grinned. "May we please have one, Ms. Dani?"

Dani fixed them both a s'more then made one for Mac. He bit into it, closed his eyes and groaned. "This is delicious."

Pleasure coursed through Dani. "Fantastic, huh?"

He stared at her mouth, his voice low. "No. Not as good as that." Grinning, he broke his s'more in two then held it out. "Here."

She took it from him and ate it slowly, licking sticky marshmallow and rich chocolate from her lips after every bite. Jaxon and the girls ate two more then grew quiet, their bellies full and eyes heavy.

"Time for y'all to crawl in your sleeping bags." Mac stood, starting toward the girls.

"Can Ms. Dani tuck us in, Dad?" Nadine asked.

Mac hesitated, surprise crossing his features. "That's up to Ms. Dani."

"Will you, Ms. Dani?" Maddie asked. "And could you maybe, braid our hair?" She bit her lip. "Just so we won't get tangles while we sleep?"

Dani's throat closed, the emotions coursing through her so strong she could barely speak. "I'd be happy to."

Maddie smiled, a look of pure joy in her eyes, and Dani swore she'd never seen anything so beautiful.

Dani spent the next hour in the tent with the girls. They took turns sitting in her lap by the lantern while she braided their long hair, their slight weight comforting. Afterward, she told a bedtime story at their request—the only one she remembered hearing from her mother during her own childhood years—until they fell asleep.

She watched them quietly for a moment, trying to envision them in New York or even a small city, away from Elk Valley. From everything they'd ever known. She tried to imagine how Jaxon would feel, leaving a ranch that held so many memories of his mother and settling somewhere strange and different. And Mac...

I can't see what I used to.

Dani squeezed her eyes shut and tried—*really tried*—to see it. To picture Mac happy somewhere else. Somewhere without the overlook. Without Sugar Falls. Somewhere besides the ranch. But all she could see was Mac chasing his girls in the field, hiking the trails with Jaxon and kissing her on the cabin deck.

What would you do, Dani, if you had to start over? Where would you go?

She wrapped her arms tight around her waist, still able to feel Mac's touch and certain, now more than ever, that she was exactly where she belonged. That Mac was, too. That no matter what happened, she wouldn't return to Vaughn Real Estate or stay in New York. Because her heart belonged in Elk Valley with Mac and his children.

Dani kissed the girls' cheeks, quietly left the tent then zipped it up.

"They asleep?" Mac stood by the fire, watching her.

She nodded. "Jaxon?"

"Knocked out." He smiled. "They had a long day."

She walked over, took his hand and pulled. "Come with me."

"What?" He followed close at her back. "Wait, where are we going?"

"Just…right…here." Dani climbed up a steep incline then stopped several feet beyond the campsite, far enough that the glow of the fire couldn't reach them. The view was clear and open and a soft breeze swept over her skin. "Perfect."

She faced Mac and closed her eyes. "Ask me what I see."

"Dani, wha—"

"Ask me."

He made a sound of amused frustration. "Your eyes are closed. You can't see anything."

She shook her head and reached for his other hand, her fingers fumbling over his abs then his hip, before catching hold of it and squeezing. "Please, Mac."

He sighed, his heavy exhale moving her hair. "What do you see?"

She focused on the dim glow behind her closed eyelids. It was so weak it was barely discernible, but it was there. "I see soft, white light. More of a glow, really.

Probably the stars." She smiled. "There are so many here. They're so close, it's like you can touch heaven."

His hands stilled in hers.

"Ask me what I hear."

His leg shifted and his boot scraped against loose rocks. "What do you hear?"

"Water moving. If you listen hard, you can hear the creek. There's this quiet rush when the water hits the rocks. And the crickets are chirping." She cocked her head, straining for more. "The leaves are rustling— the breeze is doing that. Maybe a few animals, even. They're probably roaming around, looking for a little romance."

He laughed softly. The heat of his body grew stronger as he stepped closer, his hard chest brushing hers.

"And there are crackles," she said. "Pops, too. From the campfire. Right near where Jaxon and the girls are sleeping." She released his hands and pressed her palms to his chest. Her fingers trembled and she flexed them, making them steady. "Now, ask me what I feel."

She waited, hearing the same sounds as before but not his voice. Her heart skipped painfully in her chest and she wished she could see his face. Wished she knew what he was thinking.

"Mac?"

His warm lips parted hers, his tongue sweeping inside. His fingers threaded gently through her hair. The stubble lining his jaw rasped against her cheek as he kissed her deeper, pressing his body against hers from chest to hip.

A soft moan of pleasure escaped her. His hands tightened in her hair then his thumbs rubbed the nape of her neck.

His mouth left hers, his lips touching her ear as he asked, "What do you feel?"

She pressed her cheek to his. Her skin tingled and heat swirled low in her belly. "Safe. Protected." Her blood rushed, heart pounding in her ears. "Loved."

The word lingered on her tongue and she savored it, repeating it in her head.

Loved. She loved Mac. And Jaxon. And the girls. More than she thought it was possible to love someone. And their happiness was more valuable than anything else. More than her old life and promotion in New York. Even more than the approval of her father.

So she'd help Mac in the only way she had left— by making sure he kept his land. Whatever it cost her.

Dani opened her eyes. "You told me once that a stranger wouldn't know how to protect these mountains. That they couldn't understand or properly appreciate the serenity that exists here." She cupped his jaw and met his eyes as he stared down at her. "But I do. And I can help others see the same things you and I see. Because I know you can still see it, Mac. You can still see how magnificent this place can be. If you're willing to take a chance and change some things, I can turn this place around. If you're willing to tru—" She swallowed hard, the words sticking in her throat. "If you're willing to trust me, you and the kids can still have a future here."

Mac smoothed his hands over her forearms. "What would it take?"

"A new vision." She thought of the plans she'd drawn up during her first weeks on the ranch. "One I can put together quickly that would involve renovations and enhancements. It'd take a couple weeks of hard work around the clock, all hands on deck. And a small investment. Enough to impress one large group of clients. A powerful group that I can pull strings to get here."

Mac frowned. "I have very little money left, Dani. Just some savings I tucked away for when the time came for us to move on."

"Only give me what you can spare. I'll take care of the rest."

"How?"

"I can call in a few favors."

His frown deepened. "From who?"

She wrapped her arms around him and hid her face against his throat. She couldn't tell him the whole truth. Not yet. Otherwise, he'd never agree and he'd end up losing everything.

"You just have to trust me," she said. "I can't make the decision for you, Mac. You can still leave, pack up and start over like you said. Or you can give this land one last shot at thriving. It has to be your choice. I just wanted to let you know you had one."

His chest lifted on a strong breath as he hugged her close. After a few minutes, he said, "I'll call Nate in the morning. Ask him to come out as soon as he can. If he shows, he can help with the renovations."

Dani nuzzled the smooth skin at the base of his throat, trying to focus on the task at hand and not dwell on the repercussions. She'd do everything she could to save his land and make sure he and the children kept their home. Then afterward, once he knew the truth... there was a very real chance she'd lose him.

"I won't let you down." Fresh tears burned her eyes. "I swear I won't."

He kissed the top of her head. "I trust you, Dani."

Chapter Eight

"I need a boost."

Dani looked up, her fingers pausing over her cell phone, just as Maddie started climbing up onto the window ledge. "Maddie, wait. I'll wipe the top windows."

"But I can do it if I can reach them," she said, holding her rag in one hand and pulling on the ledge with her other.

Dani tossed her cell phone on the bed and walked across the guest room, edging by Nadine as she put sheets on the mattress and Jaxon as he vacuumed the carpet.

She smiled. The children had worked hard for hours. For the past three days since they'd returned from camping, actually. They'd helped Dani clean all the guest rooms on the first floor of the lodge, were finishing up the last one on the second floor and had agreed to tackle the ones on the third floor with Dani first thing tomorrow.

Mac, Cal and Tim had stripped then polished the hard wood floors in the foyer yesterday, were completing repairs to the staircases and decks today and planned to refresh several of the cabins tomorrow. Everyone had hit the ground running and would continue to work hard until their first group of guests arrived next Friday, which left them roughly one more week to finish renovations, train the small staff on new policies and procedures and put together the most relaxing corporate retreat imaginable.

Dani cringed, her stomach churning. That was, if Scott came through on what he'd promised two days ago and Elk Valley Ranch actually had guests next week. Mac had given her a hefty portion of his savings for renovations and the only chance he had at turning a profit was a successful corporate retreat with clients willing to pay top dollar.

Oh, please, please let this work out. For Mac and the children's sake.

"Will you please let me do it?" Maddie asked, raising her voice over the noise of the vacuum and blinking up at her.

"Yes." Dani knelt and braced one hand on the window ledge. "If you climb onto my shoulders, I think you'll be able to reach the top corners."

Maddie smiled and clamored up Dani's back, her small hands and feet digging into Dani's sides.

Dani flinched and gripped the ledge tighter as Maddie straddled her shoulders. "All set up there?"

"Yep." Maddie giggled then bounced. "Beam me up, Ms. Dani."

"Oh, honey, please don't bounce. That hurts." Dani laughed then shoved to her feet, wobbling slightly as she balanced Maddie's weight in line with her own. "Okay, have at it. Just be careful and don't lean too far to the side. Let me know if you need me to move to the right or left, all right?"

"Yes, ma'am."

Dani's upper body swayed back and forth as Maddie started wiping the windows and humming.

The vacuum stopped. "I'm done," Jaxon said.

Nadine patted the pillows on the bed. "Me, too. What's next?"

"I think a break is in order," Dani said. "Thank you for working so hard. You've both done a great job."

"I'm not tired." Jaxon wound up the vacuum cleaner cord. "Want me to put some towels and soap in the bathrooms? We don't have any on this floor yet."

"I can help him," Nadine added.

"Did I just hear two of my children offer to help clean more than what they'd already agreed to?" Mac's sexy drawl filled the room as he stood in the doorway. His wide shoulders and lean hips looked even more impressive in the narrow opening. "Good Lord. This occasion calls for a calendar so I can record this for posterity."

Jaxon rolled his eyes and the girls laughed.

"Don't tease them too much," Dani said, peering around Maddie's leg and smiling at Mac. "We might lose them and we need all the help we can get."

Mac grinned, watching Maddie scrub the top edges of the window. "Things going okay in here?"

"Excellent, actually." Dani grabbed Maddie's thighs as she tottered to the side and regained her balance. "The bedrooms on the first two floors are clean and the electrician is scheduled to be here within the hour to take care of the dead outlets. I finished setting up a new router and I was just checking the signal to make sure the Wi-Fi is reaching—"

"Wi-Fi?" Mac frowned. "Internet access is set up in the great room."

"I know," Dani said calmly. "But that's a problem because guests—especially corporate ones—have grown accustomed to having access whenever and wherever they need it."

"Maybe elsewhere but not here. One of the biggest advantages of this ranch has always been the escapism it provides."

"Yes, but for some guests, it's also the ranch's biggest disadvantage. Some people don't want to work or revisit their regular lives while on vacation but some do. We need to provide the choice."

"But all this new furniture, team-building exercises and policy changes are altering everything. This isn't how we've always done it and it's a big risk."

"I understand, Mac. But we're only adding modern amenities and offering extra services. The cabins are still available for private, more rustic getaways. Only the lodge will be used to offer corporate retreats. This gets you the most return on all the ranch's potential. If we want this to be a success, we have to attract more guests. And more guests mean varied interests. So either way, we have to make the changes."

"You said *some* changes." Mac walked toward her. "Not a complete overhaul."

"Yes, and I meant it. These changes are just enhancements. Elk Valley itself will essentially remain the same."

"Like the s'mores?" Jaxon asked. "It's still our roasted marshmallow, you're just adding to it?"

Dani snapped her fingers and grinned. "That's it exactly."

Maddie lifted her leg, her knee bumping Dani's chin. "I'm ready to get down."

Dani rubbed her jaw. "All right. Hold on for a sec, please."

She backed away from the window and reached up but Mac's broad hands got there first, lifting Maddie from her shoulders and setting her down.

Dani blew a strand of hair out of her face and eyed Mac. "Look, I'd love to argue some more but this isn't a good time. The electrician will be here any minute and I need to help the kids finish restocking the bathrooms." She grabbed his hand and squeezed. "We're in this together, okay? I told you I wouldn't let you down and I meant it."

"I know. I trust you." He rubbed his forehead. "It's just that these changes are making me nervou—"

A muffled ringing started.

Mac pulled his cell phone from his pocket. "Not mine."

"It's yours, Ms. Dani." Jaxon grabbed her cell phone from the bed and glanced at the screen. "Who's Scott?"

She hesitated, feeling Mac's eyes on her, then held her hand out. "Someone from New York."

Jaxon handed her the phone.

Mac stared at the phone, a muscle ticking in his jaw. "Someone?"

Dani's finger hovered over the screen. The low tone of his voice sent flutters through her. "My brother. He's one of the people I called for a favor."

Relief flickered across his face. Catching her eyes on him, he adopted a bland expression then shrugged. "Good to know."

Dani smiled.

His lips twitched then he smiled back. "I'll go stain the front deck."

"Thank you."

He hovered, staring at her mouth, then smiled wider and left with the kids.

Shivers of pleasure chased over her skin. Good grief, he was gorgeous.

Dani took the call and pressed the phone to her ear. "Scott, please tell me you have good news."

"I have good news." She could almost hear the smile in his voice. "A group of twenty from Austin and Mills are booked next Friday for one week."

"Lawyers?" she asked.

"Every one of them." Scott laughed. "And not just any lawyers—the best ones in New York. They're fresh off an eight-month case that just wrapped up. Even the president, Jack Austin, is coming. Turns out, he's done business with Dad and said he'd be happy to do us a favor. He said his team is so wrung-out it'd take a miracle to breathe life into them."

Dani bit the inside of her cheek. "Then I guess Mac and I will have to produce a miracle."

"Dani, have you really thought this through? Dad's been asking about you and the property a lot lately. If you pull this off, he's going to lose a hell of a lot of money—"

"You haven't told him my plans, have you?"

"All I told him was that you really liked the place and had decided to stay and work on the deal for a while longer. But when he finds out what you're doing, you could lose your promotion—"

"It's not my promotion." She stood still, waiting for the familiar burn of disappointment and failure. But surprisingly, it didn't come. "It's yours. You've worked hard and you've earned it."

"So have you."

"Maybe," she whispered. "But I didn't want it for the right reasons and I don't think working in that office ever made me happy. Not really."

Dani moved to the window. The sun was out, shining brightly through the mountain mist onto the horses grazing in the green fields. She shifted onto her toes and stretched her calves, remembering the invigorating burn that had energized her muscles hiking the mountain trail. She flexed her biceps, recalling the weight of the ax in her hands as she'd swung it, feeling stronger than ever.

"What are you saying, Dani?"

She smiled. "I quit."

"What?" Scott's voice tightened. "Now, hold on a minute. You've been out there way too long and you're not seeing the big picture. When you come back, you'll feel differently."

"I'm not coming back. I'm happy here. I feel more like myself here than I have anywhere else."

Muffled voices sounded below and she looked down, watching as Mac walked out onto the front porch. He put a tray of paintbrushes on the rail and a bucket of stain on the floor then stepped back, surveying the deck.

"I'm starting over," she said firmly. She thought of Mac's reaction when she eventually told him the truth and a wave of panic turned her stomach. "Whether it's here…or somewhere else like it. I don't want to be stuck in an office pushing paper and selling property. I'd rather be outside, working the grounds. Can you imagine what that would be like? Breathing fresh air and bringing out the best in the land around you? Not answering to a board or feeling like you had to prove yourself to anyone? Just living and being accepted for who you are, flaws and all?"

Silence descended on the line then Scott said, "I imagine it would be the closest you could get to paradise."

"That's exactly what Elk Valley is," she said. "Paradise."

Mac walked back inside and Dani glanced at the staining materials then the winding driveway. No need to stand here running her mouth when she could be helping Mac and have a clear view for when the electrician arrived. It'd be a perfect opportunity to start her apology, however small that start might be. And a chance to tell him how she really felt about him so he'd understand why Elk Valley Ranch's success was as important to her as it was to him.

"I need to go, Scott." She headed for the door. "There's a lot of work to do. Thank you for your help."

She disconnected the call, shoved her phone in her pocket and went downstairs, stopping briefly to check on the kids. After helping Jaxon and the girls carry a load of towels and soap to the second floor for disbursement, she went to the front porch.

The grounds were full and busy. Several ranch hands hammered new fencing in place while others painted the stable or pressure-washed the stones in the long walkway leading to the lodge. Mac had returned to the deck and stood by the first set of steps, sweeping a paintbrush over the handrail.

Squaring her shoulders, she walked up behind him and wrapped her arms around his middle. "I'm sorry for arguing with you earlier. I don't want you to think

I'm trying to change everything or that I don't love what you have here. And we do need to talk at some point. There are things I need to tell you. You see, I... I lied to you when I first met you. I'm not exactly the person I said I was and I didn't come here for the same reasons that I'm staying." He stiffened and she lifted to her toes, her heart pounding painfully as she whispered in his ear, "But the truth is, I do love it here— love *you*, actually." She swallowed hard, rushing out, "And I want others to see Elk Valley the way we see it. Like the overlook or Sugar Falls. Even with that broken deck, that waterfall was one of the most beautiful things I'd ever seen." She laughed softly. "I don't know. Maybe it was only because I was in your arms but it was magic. Don't you remember how that felt?"

"Nope." He swiveled in her arms and faced her, a crooked grin appearing. "Remind me. What'd we do up on that deck all by ourselves?"

Dani stilled, her hands pressed to his wide chest. He felt different. And she felt different around him. He was still as handsome as ever but something was... off. Enough so, that it overcame the clamoring nerves that had assaulted her when she'd said she loved him.

She studied his smile, which tipped at a new angle and there was a mischievous gleam in his eyes that hadn't been there before. Her focus dropped to his shirt—a buttoned Western-style, one he hadn't been wearing earlier.

"Did you change your clothes?" she asked.

"Today?" At her nod, he said, "Yep. As I do every day."

"And your hair." She reached up and sifted her fingers through the tousled strands, which stood out at odd—but attractive—angles. "It looks..."

"More modern? Stylish?" He cut his eyes to the left, grinning wider. "I'm a great guy but in case you haven't noticed, I can be pretty uptight and predictable. Thought it was time I loosened up a bit. Got a little more spontaneous—"

"What the hell, Nate?"

Dani started and looked over her shoulder. Mac—*another one?*—stood at the other end of the deck. Except this Mac, even angry, had the ability to warm her insides and melt her heart. Scowling, he stared at her hands, one of which rested on the man's chest in front of her and the other, still lingering in his hair.

"Hold up there, bro. I didn't do a thing but play along." Smiling, Nate spread his arms and nodded toward a bulky overnight bag on the porch steps. "I got your voice mail, came on out and was simply helping fix up the place when a beautiful woman showed up and accosted me." He shrugged. "Not that I'm complaining or anything—"

"Oh, God." Dani snatched her hands from his chest and stumbled back, pressing her palms to her scorching cheeks. This was *Nate*. Mac's brother. And she'd told him she'd lied to Mac. That she *loved* him. *"Oh, G—"*

"Don't worry," Nate said, grin returning. "Your secrets are safe with me." He winked. "For now."

Mac stalked toward them. "What secrets?"

"Nothing. Just some commentary she thought she was sharing with you before I had a chance to tell her who I was." Nate cocked an eyebrow, expression serious. "Although, I'm gonna tell you both right now that you'll just have to find some other deck to canoodle on.

Sugar Falls has the best fishing hole on the ranch and I plan to spend my off-hours up there catching trout."

Dani pried her dry tongue from the roof of her mouth and turned to Mac. "Why didn't you tell me you had an identical twin?"

Mac gripped her hip and tugged her to his side. "It didn't seem important at the time and I didn't expect him to pop up out of nowhere."

"You said you needed help so I came as quickly as I could." Nate narrowed his eyes. "Didn't think I had to call and ask permission before I came home."

"You don't," Mac said, voice heavy. "It just would've been nice to know you were on the way so you didn't take anyone by surprise."

The brothers eyed each other and Mac's hold on Dani's hip tightened.

Nate laughed, brows raising. "Well now, this is new. Haven't seen this side of you before, man."

Mac released her hip and a small smile crossed his face. "Maybe if you came home more often, you would."

"So you did miss me, huh?" Nate asked, grinning.

Mac laughed. "Maybe."

"You know you did."

"Nate, this is Dani Jones," Mac said. "She's heading up the renovations around here."

Nate tossed the paintbrush on the rail and held out his hand. "Nice to meet you."

Dani shook his hand and avoided his eyes, a bead of sweat trickling over her temple. "Nice to meet you, too."

He smiled at her then turned to Mac. "I can see you've got enough help here, so I'll find Cal and lend a hand elsewhere. Though I'd like to see my two beautiful nieces and cool nephew before I get started. Where are they?"

Mac gestured toward the front door. "Inside, second floor. And Nate? Thanks for coming. I know it probably cost you this time of year and I appreciate it."

Nate paused on the threshold, his carefree grin faltering. "All you ever had to do was ask, Mac."

After Nate left, Dani slumped back against the wall. "That was so embarrassing. I honestly thought he was you at first."

Mac rubbed his hands over her upper arms, a rueful expression crossing his face. "Sorry about that. Old habits die hard, it seems. Used to, we got a kick out of pretending to be each other." He shrugged. "I didn't expect him to come home this soon—if at all."

Dani frowned. "What did you mean when you said you knew it would cost him to come here?"

"Money. The circuit's busy during the summer and I'm sure he had to ditch several competitions to help me out. Nate rarely comes home and it's usually never of his own volition. We haven't been all that close, lately. He likes chasing bulls too much." He grimaced. "And women. Which may have been one reason why I overreacted just now."

The sour note in his voice made her smile. He'd had the same look on his face when Scott had called. "So this other side of you—the one he's never seen," she prompted. "Which side might that be?"

He smiled then kissed her gently. "The jealous one." His lips moved against hers as he asked, "And those secrets he mentioned. Which ones might those be?"

Her heart kicked her ribs. *That I'm not perfect. That*

I messed up, but I love you. That I hope you'll be able to forgive me.

She cupped his jaw and pressed her forehead to his, the truth and lies tangling so tight in her throat she could barely breathe. "We can talk about it later," she said. "Right now, let's work on saving your ranch."

Chapter Nine

Mac slipped a finger under the collar of his T-shirt and tugged. Damn, it was hot. Too hot to be standing outside on the deck, waiting for a load of lawyers to arrive.

Tim nudged him with an elbow, shifting from one boot to the other at his left. "They were supposed to be here half an hour ago. Think they got lost?"

Mac rubbed the knot at the base of his neck and peered down the long driveway. Not a car in sight. "Could be."

"Could be they stopped to stretch their legs or something," Nate said at his side, staring at the driveway. "It's a damned long trip from New York."

"Could be they're just not gonna show," Cal said, walking up behind them. He plucked a bright strawberry from the plate in his hand and popped it in his mouth. "Might have decided to go to some fancy hotel instead."

"They didn't change their mind," Mac said, though the possibility had occurred to him more than once. Taking the plate from Cal, he shook his head. "Didn't you hear Dani say these were reserved for guests?"

"Yeah, Cal. They're for guests." Nate reached over, snagged a strawberry and took a bite. He groaned, clearly enjoying it, before saying, "And stop looking at me like that, Mac. Technically, since you invited me, I'm your guest."

Mac cocked an eyebrow. "Really? You didn't seem like a guest last night when you were barking orders at me."

"I wasn't barking orders at you. I was just offering advice on how to mow the fields properly and make a good first impression. Look at that." He gestured toward the neatly manicured grass beside the driveway. "Look at those beautiful straight lines. There's no way you would've pulled that off on your own."

Mac smiled. "Oh, yeah?"

"Yeah." Nate went for another strawberry.

Mac covered the plate with his hand and bit back a laugh. "Leave the damned strawberries alone. And you're not a guest, you're family."

Nate flashed that cocky grin of his and pressed a hand to his chest. "You hear that, boys? My brother just admitted out loud, to God and everyone, that we're related. Things are looking up for me."

Mac shook his head. "Things would always look up for you if you'd stay in one place for more than a week at a time."

"Well, count 'em." He held up two fingers. "I've been here for almost two weeks now."

"I know." Mac smiled, recalling the dozens of piggyback rides Nate had given the girls and the several trips he'd taken with Jaxon to the fishing hole at Sugar Falls. "Wish you'd think about staying a while longer. The kids have been in hog heaven having you around again."

Nate sobered and shoved his hands in his pockets.

"I've missed 'em. They've grown so much since I last saw them."

Mac eyed him, noting the slight sag of his shoulders and closed expression. He'd been gone for more than seven months this time out, moving from one competition to another. He'd looked tired when he'd arrived—exhausted, even. So much so, it worried him. And he'd forgotten how good it felt to have his brother back.

"This is still your home, Nate." Mac bit his tongue. "At least…until the bank takes it."

Nate looked up, his smile returning. "That's not going to happen. Dani's too ambitious and you're too stubborn. After all the work you've put in sprucing this place up, there's no way this ranch won't turn a profit."

"We," Mac stressed. "We did this." He glanced at Cal and Tim. "All of us."

They'd worked their tails off overhauling this place and it'd never looked better. Every one of Dani's ideas had pulled together better than he'd hoped. Now all they needed were customers.

Mac cringed and grabbed a strawberry, biting into it nervously. "Let's just hope they show."

"They're here," Dani said, walking swiftly onto the deck. "The driver just called and said they're turning onto the driveway now."

She carried a tray filled with glasses of lemonade, ice clinking in the glasses while the kids followed close behind her. Jaxon and the girls carried baskets of fresh fruit, excited looks on their faces.

Dani stopped, looked at the half-eaten strawberry in his hand and frowned. "Mac, I said those were for guests."

"I tried to tell him that," Nate drawled.

Mac rolled his eyes and smiled. "Yeah. It's just like old times having you back, Nate."

"I told you you missed me." He laughed then headed down the walkway with Cal, Tim and the kids, saying over his shoulder, "Keep him straight, Dani."

Dani smiled back at Nate. Friendly but reserved. And without the bright look in her eyes Mac had grown accustomed to.

He set the plate of strawberries aside, wondering what was up between her and Nate. They'd gotten along well over the past week and a half but he'd noticed Dani didn't behave like herself around his brother. She was more quiet than usual and it seemed to be more than just residual embarrassment from their first awkward encounter. And Nate, uncharacteristically serious in tone, had begun fishing for information, asking Mac how he and Dani had met and where she was from.

Mac frowned. What had she said to Nate that day that made her so uncomfortable? On more than one occasion, he'd asked Nate but he'd been no help. Nate just brushed him off, saying it wasn't his place to share and he was sure she'd get around to telling him herself. Which made him think it might have been too personal to repeat.

"Are you nervous?"

Mac glanced up, taking in Dani's shaky smile and cute look of concern.

"Because there's no reason to be." She rose on her tiptoes, balancing the tray of drinks carefully, and kissed his cheek. "Just be you. Wonderful, fantastic you. And they'll love this place as much as I do."

Her words were solid. But he noticed the slight tremble in her arms, and her chest lifted against his arm with rapid breaths.

Something shifted in his chest as he considered the possibilities. Clearly, she was worried, too. But she was standing by his side, reinventing Elk Valley Ranch, hoping for the best and attempting to support him through the potential worst should it happen. As though she might feel as strongly for him as he had for her. It had certainly felt that way at the overlook when she'd used the word *love*.

He helped her balance the tray with one hand and caressed her nape with the other. "You remember what you said last week? About us being in this together?"

She nodded, relaxing beneath his touch.

The feel of her silky skin and supportive presence soothed him on the inside, slipping into his veins and making his heart swell within his chest. Just as it had for weeks now.

It hit him hard then. How happy Jaxon was playing baseball with her in the field in the afternoons. How much the girls smiled when she read them bedtime stories and braided their hair. And how much he looked forward to seeing her face each morning, realizing that every day he spent with her filled him up more on the inside. In a way Nicole never had.

The bittersweet thought shot a bolt of pain through him, leaving a guilty trail in its wake. But despite it, he couldn't stop the next words from pushing past his lips.

"Us," he whispered. "I like the sound of that."

Her lips parted as she looked up at him, her cheeks turning a pretty pink. "Me, too."

An engine rumbled across the valley, pulling his focus from her. Two stretch limos appeared, moving slowly down the slope of the last hill, then drew to a stop in front of the lodge. Cal, Tim and Nate walked to the driveway and smoothed a hand over their collars and belts. The girls set their baskets aside and ran up to one of the limos, cupping their hands and peering in the tinted windows.

"Girls, stop that," Nate said. He and Tim scrambled after them as they ran to the next limo, laughing.

"Dad," Jaxon shouted. "Nadine and Maddie are going to scare them off."

"Hope you got enough lemonade," Cal said, glancing up at them. "It's hot as blazes out here."

Mac looked at Dani, finding the same apprehension he felt reflected in her eyes.

"Well," he said, digging deep for what he hoped was a sincere smile. "Looks like they just got their Elk Valley welcome, so let's get this party started."

ONE WEEK, SIX HIKES, seven trail rides and ten team-building sessions later, Jack Austin and his team packed their bags, ate dinner in Elk Valley Ranch's banquet hall then headed back to New York. On the way out, Jack handed Mac a check for an amount so big he had to sit down and double-check the figure twice.

"You sure he made that out right?" Nate asked, leaning across the banquet hall table and studying the check.

"Yep," Mac said. "He handed it to me at the door. Told me it included gratuity."

Nate's brow furrowed. "But I thought you and Dani included that in the original quote."

"We did." Mac smiled, glancing at Dani as she and the kids cleared the dirty dishes from another table then walked into the back kitchen. "He said he didn't think I was charging enough, so he increased it."

Nate sat back in his chair. "Well, damn. We actually managed to pull this off, huh?"

Mac nodded slowly. "Enough to hold the bank off for another month or two. And that's not even the best part." He retrieved a piece of paper from his pocket and held it up, tapping the name scrawled in ink toward the bottom. "Jack mentioned he recommended us to a few of his friends and Ann said she already got a call from one of them this morning. Said the guy's secretary asked if he could stop by Monday morning to take a look around before reserving."

Nate leaned closer and read the name. "Daniel Vaughn."

"Yep. And something tells me that if he's a friend of Jack's, he must have money." Mac put the paper back in his pocket. "Something we definitely still need."

The double doors to the kitchen swung open and Dani and the kids walked out with empty trays, ready to clean off another table.

"Hold up," Mac said, jumping to his feet and crossing the room. "You four have cleaned enough tonight and I just gave everyone else the night off." He took the trays then stacked them on the table. "Nate and I will take care of the rest."

"Did they like the place, Dad?" Jaxon asked.

Mac nodded. "They sure did. We've got another big spender stopping by Monday to take a look at the place and more guests than usual just checked in this morning, which means business is looking up."

Dani moved close and whispered, "Did you make enough to get by another month or two?"

Mac smiled. "Yeah. And possibly a third."

Her eyes lit up and she clasped her hands together, laughing. "That's wonderful."

"I think this calls for a celebration," Mac said. "Maybe we could give the new guests something special and have a dance tomorrow night, here in the banquet hall, around eight?"

The girls whooped and started dancing, their blond curls bouncing.

Mac glanced at Nate. "You up for a party? We all deserve a night of fun and it'd give the staff a chance to run through a formal event for the first time. They'll need the extra training if the guests keeping pouring in."

"I'm down with that." Nate stood then walked over and hugged Nadine and Maddie. "Just as long as my two favorite girls save me a dance."

"Sure will." Nadine grinned at Dani. "You gonna save Dad a dance, Ms. Dani?"

Mac waited, a slow heat building within him as Dani ran her eyes over him.

"There's a good chance I will," she said, smiling.

"I certainly hope so." Mac glanced at his watch. "All right, kids. It's time y'all head back to the lodge and wash up."

"I'll take them," Dani said. "Come on, guys."

The three of them headed out the door and Dani followed.

Mac watched her walk away, visualizing how long the walk was from the lodge to her cabin. There were eight hundred and sixty-two steps from his front door to hers. He'd counted during his walk to see her yesterday morning, hating how much distance was still between them.

Catching up with her, he took her hand and tugged her close. "Why don't you stay at the lodge with us tonight instead of going back to the cabin?"

She hesitated, blinking up at him in surprise.

He bit his lip and looked over his shoulder. Nate had his back to them, collecting dirty dishes. "I mean, we have all those updated rooms and two of them are empty at the moment."

A teasing light entered her eyes and she whispered, "Is that the only reason?"

He laughed. "For tonight, yeah." He leaned down and brushed his lips across her cheek. "You'd be closer to us and it'd sure be nice to see you first thing in the morning."

Her thumb smoothed across his wrist, making him weak at the knees. God help him, he wanted her hands on him. Wanted his ring on her finger. Wanted her beside him every night and in his life every day.

"I'd like that," she said. "Good night, Mac."

He bent his head and kissed her, savoring the soft feel of her mouth beneath his and the pleasurable throb in his chest. "Good night."

He waited until she walked through the door and out of sight, then returned to the table and started stacking dirty dishes.

Nate paused beside him, forks clutched in his hand. "In the two weeks I've been here, you've basically overhauled the ranch, led team-building exercises—which, by the way, I never thought I'd see you do—and now, you're about to wash dirty dishes." He whistled long and low. "You've got it bad, brother."

Mac's hands stilled on the tray, that familiar pang of discomfort returning. "Yeah. I do."

Nate dropped the forks on the tray and started gathering up glasses. "You say that like it's a bad thing."

"Maybe it is."

"How so? She's single, you're single—"

"I wasn't always." Mac tightened his grip on the tray, feeling Nate's eyes on him. "You know I was going to leave with you that day, right? That if Nicole hadn't been pregnant with Jaxon, I would've left Elk Valley years ago. Even if she decided not to."

Nate nodded slowly.

"I loved Nicole. I swear I did." He blinked hard and shoved his hands in his pockets. "It was both our faults. We both put ourselves in that position. But I..." He gritted his teeth. "I resented not having the choice. And then I think of what my life would be like without Jaxon and—"

His voice broke and he looked away, focusing on the dark night outside the window.

"And you feel guilty?" Nate asked.

"Yeah." He swallowed hard. "And it's not just that. A while back, Maddie asked me if I still loved Nicole. I told her I did and that was true to a certain extent. But what I have with Dani is different. I don't know if it's because I was still so young when I met Nicole. That maybe that's why everything feels so different with Dani. So new and powerful." His throat closed. "I want Dani in my life but it's not just me. Everything I do has an impact on Jaxon, Nadine and Maddie. I'd be taking a risk for them as much as for myself."

"Almost everything in life is a risk," Nate said softly. "Just look at what you and Dani have done with this place. How you took a chance and brought it back to life." He gripped his shoulder and squeezed. "Everyone has regrets, Mac. You're a great dad. Wanting Dani in your life doesn't mean you're being disloyal to your kids and you're not betraying Nicole by moving on. It's okay to live again. To love again. Nicole would've wanted that."

Mac faced him then, his chest burning as he searched Nate's eyes. "But I love Dani more."

"More than Nicole?"

Mac forced himself to say it. Out loud. "Yeah."

Nate smiled. "That's okay, too."

Chapter Ten

Mac grabbed his cologne and sprayed it lightly over the base of his throat then behind his ear, smiling as Jaxon stared up at him.

"Can I have some?"

Mac cocked an eyebrow. "Why? You got a hot date tonight?"

Jaxon rolled his eyes and laughed. "No. I just wanted to try it." He leaned on the bathroom sink, fiddling with Mac's razor. "When can I start shaving?"

"That'll be a while yet. But I'll show you when the time comes." He held up the cologne bottle. "Come here. I'll spritz you."

Jaxon scooted closer and raised his chin, exposing his neck.

Mac laughed and sprayed him once. "There. You're good to go."

He hoped they both were. It'd been so long since he'd been on a date, he'd almost forgotten what one was. He guessed he could call dancing with Dani in the banquet hall a date. Hell, he didn't care what it was called so long as he was able to spend time with her. He hadn't been able to think of anything else since he kissed her last night.

Well…except for his conversation with Nate. That was something he'd revisited more than once throughout the day, weighing the risks versus rewards of telling Dani how he felt. And he'd finally come to a decision.

"Is it okay if I ask a girl to dance?"

Mac refocused on Jaxon. "Which girl?"

Jaxon shrugged. "Laura, maybe."

Mac grinned. Along with the dozen or so guests, he and Nate had invited several friends to the dance tonight. Laura was the daughter of one of Nate's friends. A nice kid, around Jaxon's age.

"Yeah. That'd be perfectly fine."

Jaxon frowned. "But…but what if she says no?"

"There's always a chance of that," Mac said, tapping his chin. "But you'll never know if you don't ask. And if you really like her, it'll be worth the risk."

Almost everything in life is a risk. Mac rolled his shoulders, recalling Nate's words, and decided there was no better time than the present to take the first step.

"How 'bout we go find your sisters and have a quick chat before we head to the dance?"

Jaxon nodded and they walked down the hall to the girls' room.

Once there, Mac knocked on the door. "Are you ready, girls? I'd like to talk to you before we head out."

There were muffled giggles and a scuffling sound then Nadine opened the door. She wore a green dress and her hair was brushed neatly, falling in shiny curls around her smiling face.

"Like my hair?" she asked. "Ms. Dani did it."

Mac grinned and wound his finger through one of her curls. "It's beautiful, baby."

"She did mine, too." Maddie skipped out of the en suite bathroom, her skirt fluttering around her knees, and held out her hands. "And she painted our nails."

He smoothed his thumb over the glittery polish and chuckled. "Green?"

"No. Mint Breeze." Dani stood in the bathroom doorway, smiling. "They asked for something besides pink and that shade matches their dresses."

Mac stilled as his eyes drifted over her. The sleeveless dress she wore hugged her curves and the dark blue material deepened the tone of her eyes to a hypnotic midnight blue. Her wavy hair spilled over her bare shoulders, making his fingers tingle with the need to touch her.

"I hope you don't mind." Her hands twisted at her waist and her tone was uncertain.

"No." He peeled his eyes from the sleek length of her legs and focused on her face. "It's beautiful."

Pink stained her cheeks and her mouth parted on a swift breath, the soft sound making his blood rush. "I'll just…go ahead and make sure everything's set up," she said, easing past the girls and heading for the door.

Mac slowed her steps with a hand on her elbow then escorted her to the hallway. "Jaxon, wait in there with the girls for a minute, okay?"

Jaxon grinned. "Sure."

Mac closed the door behind him then pulled Dani close. The soft material of her dress glided against his palm. "I know it's usually customary for the kiss to come at the end of a date but I don't think I can wait that long."

She smiled and stepped closer, tracing the curve

of his bottom lip with her finger. "Is that what this is? A date?"

He nudged her mouth with his, whispering, "Okay. We'll go with that."

Laughing softly, she kissed him. Her hands smoothed up his chest then into his hair. The tips of her nails grazed his scalp gently, sending shivers down his spine.

He wrapped his arms around her and deepened the kiss, wishing they had more time. Hoping that by the end of the night, she'd give him forever.

Mac raised his head and drew in a ragged breath. "If we don't stop now, we won't make it to the party."

Her forehead dropped to his chest on a frustrated moan. "But you smell so good."

He laughed and kissed the top of her head. "All part of the plan, babe. I'm using every trick in the book to pull you in."

She looked up and her teasing expression dimmed. "I don't think you could pull me in any more than I already am." Her fingers picked at the buttons on his shirt. "Can we talk tonight? After the dance? There are things I need to tell you."

"That's exactly what I had in mind. For the most part, at least." He kissed her once more then smiled, moving away reluctantly. "I better get back before the kids get antsy. We'll meet you down there shortly."

He watched her leave then smoothed a hand through his hair and entered the bedroom.

Jaxon sat on the edge of one of the twin beds with Nadine on one side of him and Maddie on the other. All three of them were grinning from ear to ear.

Mac's mouth quirked. "What are y'all up to?"

The girls giggled. Jaxon shrugged.

"All right," Mac said, rubbing his hands together. "Let's have that talk."

"Is it about Ms. Dani?" Jaxon asked.

Maddie bounced on the bed. "Are you still gonna dance with her?"

"Can we take Ms. Dani camping again?" Nadine asked. "I bet she likes to fish."

"Whoa. Hold up a minute." Mac edged his way onto the bed beside Nadine, freezing as it creaked beneath the four of them. When nothing gave way, he smiled, propped his elbows on his knees and looked at the three of them. "Jaxon's right. I do want to talk to you about Ms. Dani. Is it safe for me to assume that all of you are still fond of her?"

Jaxon nodded. "You know we like her, Dad."

"I know," he said, glancing from one smiling face to the next. "But I know how much she cares about you and I thought I'd touch base with you again to see if you still feel the same way about her."

Nadine's hand shot out and wrapped around his forearm. "Is she gonna stay? For good?"

Mac hesitated. He had every intention of being honest with all three of them but how much should he actually share? Falling in love again was new enough, let alone figuring out how to merge his romantic life with that of being a single father. And though he knew Dani cared for him, he still wasn't certain how she'd respond when he—

"Dad?" Maddie leaned over Jaxon, staring up at him. "Did your heart grow?"

Mac clenched his hands together between his knees, unsure of how to answer.

Jaxon's eyes clouded with confusion. "What's she talking about?"

"She's talking about how I feel about Ms. Dani." His neck heated and he cleared his throat. "I do feel strongly for her. Just like the three of you do."

They grew quiet. Jaxon sat up straighter, Maddie twisted the ribbon on her dress around her finger and Nadine stared thoughtfully at the wall.

"I've always been honest with you and I'm asking how you feel about her because I'm thinking about the future." He leaned closer, studying their expressions. "What if Ms. Dani stayed for good, like Nadine said? But not just as a hand. More like a partner."

Nadine frowned. "A partner? Will she work in the office with Ms. Ann?"

Mac laughed. "No. Not like Ms. Ann. *Our* partner. Possibly, a part of our family."

Jaxon's face brightened. "Are y'all gonna get married?"

The girls' heads jerked up and they stared at his face.

"I don't know yet," Mac said gently. "I haven't asked her but I've thought about it. And I wondered how the three of you would feel about it if I did."

"I'd like it," Jaxon said, smiling.

Mac nodded. "Nadine? What about you?"

"Sounds good to me." She grinned. "She brushes hair a lot better than Ms. Ann and tells good stories at bedtime."

"Maddie?" Mac waited, holding his breath as she stopped twisting the ribbon.

"Do you like her a lot?" she asked.

Mac bit his lip and decided honesty was the only way to go. "I love her, Maddie."

She blushed. A big smile spread across her face as she whispered, "I do, too."

Mac breathed a sigh of relief, excited about the possibilities and feeling more alive than ever. Maddie climbed into his lap and hugged his neck. Jaxon and Nadine followed, piling onto one another and throwing their arms around him, all smiles. He chuckled, struggling to wrap his arms around all three of them.

A loud pop sounded then the bed fell, tumbling them onto their backs in a heap on the floor.

Winded, Mac stayed still for a few moments then asked, "Everyone all right?"

The kids burst out laughing and Mac dropped his head back to the floor, joining them.

Jaxon pushed up on his palms and smiled. "Guess we'll have to fix that too, Dad."

THE WORLD SPUN then turned upside down. Dani gasped, her hair sweeping the dance floor, heart pounding in her ears and blood rushing straight to her cheeks.

And, dear God, she loved it.

"Damn, you're beautiful."

She opened her eyes, barely catching the words over the blare of the music. Mac leaned over her, his strong arm wrapped tight around her back, big palm cupping her head and a devilish smile on his handsome face.

Belly dipping just as quickly as he'd dipped her, she grinned. "You're not so bad yourself."

"Is that all?" He frowned in mock affront. "Then I'll just have to do something different to impress you."

His mouth—that wickedly skillful, delicious mouth

of his—planted firmly against hers. The heavy throb of bass pounded through the banquet hall floor, traveled past her curled toes up to her chest, then mingled with the vibration of Mac's groan of pleasure against her lips. Dani spread her hands across his broad shoulders and kissed him back for all she was worth.

Dimly, the sound of applause broke through her passion-induced stupor and Mac released her mouth, straightening and drawing her up with him.

A group of guests had formed a circle around them on the dance floor. They clapped and cheered, the encouraging shouts peppered with wolf whistles. The kids stood among them with Nate at their side. Even Cal and Tim had joined the fun, sipping beers and smiling. Dani laughed and buried her face against Mac's warm throat.

Mac hugged her close then led her off the dance floor. "Guess we should cool things off before they get out of hand." He nuzzled her temple and spoke softly in her ear. "Though I wouldn't mind picking this back up in private later."

She wrapped her arms around his waist and squeezed. "I wouldn't mind that, either."

He stopped and cupped her face, smiling down at her. "I'm gonna hold you to that."

"Please do."

His eyes darkened. "You have no idea how much I want to—"

"Dad, it's my turn."

Mac jumped, hands tightening around her and eyes slowly closing.

Dani peeked around his shoulder to find Nadine tugging at his pants pocket.

"You promised you were gonna dance with me next, so come on." Smiling, she yanked harder. "Make him dance with me, Ms. Dani."

Dani laughed and pushed Mac toward her. "I think you better keep your promise before you get in trouble."

"Oh, I always keep my promises." He leaned over and kissed her neck. "And I'm coming back, so don't you dare move."

He returned to the dance floor with Nadine, lifted her high in his arms and started spinning through the crowd. The sight took Dani's breath away.

She pressed a hand to her chest, her skin moist with sweat and her pulse pounding beneath her fingertips. He was so wonderful. Every moment with him reinforced how much she loved him. And every second without him reminded her how painful it would be to lose him.

Her stomach roiled. She had to tell him everything. As soon as possible.

"I taught him everything he knows." Nate appeared at her side, grinning. He nudged her with his elbow then lifted a glass of wine. "Need a drink?"

Seeking a distraction, she took it with shaky fingers and drank deeply. The tangy liquid tickled her throat, making her cough.

"Slow down, there," Nate said, patting her back. "I was trying to help, not make it worse."

Dani regained her composure and blinked away a sheen of tears. "What were you trying to help exactly?"

"That guilty conscience of yours."

She almost choked again. "Wh-what?"

"Easy," he said calmly. "I haven't given you up, yet, have I?"

"On which part?"

His brows rose. "How many parts are there?"

Dani winced. "Too many."

She craned her neck, sifting visually through the dancing couples. Mac and Nadine reappeared, still twirling and laughing.

"Why haven't you given me up?" she asked.

"I'm not one to judge. And for what it's worth, I do believe you love him." Nate glanced down at her and frowned. "But you need to come clean with whatever it is you lied to him about. The sooner, the better."

"I know." Her fingers tightened around the glass, the condensation cold against her palm. "But I don't want to hurt him."

"No way around that now, I'm afraid. And the longer you wait, the worse it'll get." He shook his head. "Mac can be stubborn. Real stubborn. Especially if he feels betrayed."

His jaw clenched and a muscle ticked by his mouth. "Do you know this from personal experience?"

He took the glass from her and tossed it back, draining the wine from it. "Yep. So just take my word for it."

"Nate." A pretty blonde, wearing glasses and a big smile, walked over. "Landon told me you were back in town but I didn't believe him."

Nate dipped his head briefly, shifting from one boot to the other. "Dani, this is Amber Eason. Her older brother, Landon, owns the ranch a few miles up the road. He went to school with me and Mac."

Dani shook Amber's hand, noticing Nate visibly growing tenser by her side as they chatted.

Amber returned her attention to Nate. "Care to dance?"

Nate lifted his chin and cast his eyes over the crowd behind her. "Depends. Where's Landon?"

"Landon's my brother, Nate. Not my father." Her smile faded. "If you don't want to dance, just say so."

Nate froze, a slow smile spreading across his face. "When'd you get so sassy?"

Amber shrugged. "While you were gone. Don't worry about it," she said, spinning away. "I'll ask someone else."

Nate sprang after her. "Now, hold up there." He stopped, turned and shoved the wineglass back into Dani's hands. "Mind holding on to that for me?"

"Sure," Dani said, but he was already escorting Amber to the center of the dance floor.

She laughed and shook her head, watching every female head within Nate's immediate vicinity turn in his direction. But his eyes were focused solely on Amber.

Twenty minutes later, the small crowd parted and Mac emerged, holding Maddie and Nadine's hands with Jaxon trailing close behind. The girls smiled but their eyes were heavy and the spring in Jaxon's step had slowed.

"It's getting late and these three started looking droopy," Mac said, stopping in front of her. He smiled and added, "Think it's time I took 'em up to bed. Nate said he'd handle wrapping things up here. Want to walk with us?"

Dani put the glass on the table and took Jaxon's hand. "Lead the way."

They strolled up the dirt path from the banquet hall to the lodge. The moon was full, lighting their way, and the muffled music from the party eventually faded, giving way to the chirping of crickets and croaks of bullfrogs.

Once they reached the family floor of the lodge, Mac nudged the kids ahead then whispered over his shoulder, "I'll get them in bed then meet you in my room in ten, okay?"

Dani nodded then made her way to Mac's bedroom. She entered slowly and hovered by the door, flicking the light on.

The room, like the rest of the lodge, was beautiful and spacious. Thick wood beams supported the high ceiling, and large windows cloaked with floor-length curtains lined the far wall. A stone fireplace faced a king-size bed on an opposing wall and a wide cherry dresser sat beside it.

She walked across the hardwood floor to the dresser and smiled, letting her fingers drift over a pair of Mac's sunglasses, a small pile of coins and the weather-beaten watch he wore when he worked. She moved further down the dresser and a flash of light, bouncing off a silver picture frame, caught her eye. Stopping, she lifted the frame and studied the photograph.

A woman smiled back at her, her long brown hair straight and sleek, her cheek pressed to Mac's. Her arms were looped loosely around his shoulders and her manicured nails rested on his broad chest—a deep pink, just as the girls had described.

Nicole.

Dani's throat tightened. She touched a fingertip to Mac's smile. They both looked so young. So happy. And Nicole was more gorgeous than Dani had imagined.

She drew in a shaky breath, her cheeks growing wet

as she stared at Mac's wife, an unwelcome stab of envy piercing her. Mac deserved to be this happy again. Deserved to be able to love a woman he could trust implicitly. A woman who wouldn't deceive him as she had.

"Dani."

She froze. The door thudded shut then Mac's footsteps approached.

"I was just—" She winced at the hoarse sound of her voice, her hands trembling around the frame. "I'm sorry. I was just looking around and saw it. I didn't mean to intrude."

His big palm covered hers, tugging the frame from her.

"She was beautiful." Dani looked down and twisted her hands, trying to still them. "And Jaxon looks so much like her. You must have loved her very much."

His arm brushed her middle as he reached out and pulled a drawer open. He placed the picture, facedown, on the bottom then pushed it shut.

His hands cupped her hips, tugging her around to face him. "Look at me."

She swallowed hard against the knot in her throat and lifted her head. His green eyes examined her face then he brushed his lips across her cheek, his tongue touching her tears. He followed their trail to the corner of her mouth, kissing her softly and cradling her face in his hands.

His low voice moved over her, his broad chest vibrating against hers. "You're the most beautiful woman I've ever met. Inside and out."

Pleasure stole through her and settled right beside the pain.

He smiled. "I've never loved a woman as much as I love you."

She melted against him, her hands curling tight into his shirt. "I love you, too."

Weaving her fingers through his hair, she pulled his mouth back down to hers. His tongue parted her lips and delved inside, sweeping softly against hers. Her heart pounded painfully in her chest and she struggled to find the words. The ones she needed to say before this went any further.

His callused fingers slipped beneath the thin straps of her dress and slid them slowly over her shoulders then down her arms. Her skin heated beneath his touch.

"Mac. I need to…"

He tugged her dress down to her waist then unclasped her bra, baring her breasts. Lowering his head, he kissed the hollow at the base of her throat then followed the curves of each breast. His mouth continued caressing, enveloping a hardened peak and drawing deeply.

Crying out softly, she tipped her head back and cupped his face. The muscles of his strong jaw moved rhythmically against her fingers, sending another wave of heat through her.

"Mac, please."

He stilled against her then raised his head and focused on her face. "Do you want me to stop?"

She smoothed her thumb over his reddened mouth, preparing to deliver the truth. To explain. To beg for forgiveness. But the thought of hurting him…

And the thought of him stopping—of his warm, solid strength leaving her—was too painful to face.

"No." She shook her head. "I don't want you to stop."

He lowered his blond head back to her breasts, then removed the rest of her clothing, his mouth tasting each inch of skin he exposed. She did the same for him, her palms smoothing over his broad chest, lean hips and muscled buttocks.

He moaned then wrapped his arms around her, lifting her against him and walking them to the bed. Covering her, he nudged her thighs apart then pressed his hips against hers. She wrapped her legs around his waist and welcomed him in, his hard body stretching hers tenderly and filling her completely.

His broad chest brushed against her breasts with each of his gentle movements and his mouth returned to hers, tasting and teasing.

Dani hugged him close and her body tightened around him, the emotions he stirred within her building so much she couldn't contain them. He joined her, his muscular frame shuddering against her, then rolled to his side and took her with him.

He tucked her head beneath his chin and she pressed her cheek to his chest.

"You were right," he whispered.

Her heart still beat heavily in her chest and she took a moment to catch her breath. "About what?"

He kissed her forehead, his lips smiling against her skin. "You fit perfectly…right here."

She closed her eyes and pressed tighter against him, wanting to stay there forever.

His legs entwined with hers and his hands smoothed over her back in large circles. Eventually, his arms relaxed around her and his breathing grew deep and even.

Dani listened to the strong beat of his heart beneath her cheek. She thought of how sweet the air was in Elk

Valley. How it filled her lungs and renewed her mind when she played baseball in the field with Jaxon. And she thought of Nadine and Maddie, recalling how comforting the girls' weight felt propped against her chest when she read to them in bed.

Her arms tightened around Mac, the fear of hurting them—of losing them—making her tremble. A phrase, repeatedly stabbing her on the inside, fought its way to her lips.

"Please forgive me."

Chapter Eleven

Mac blinked then stretched, satisfaction coursing through his veins and the distant echo of lively music looping in his mind.

"Mmm."

Dani.

His arms stilled over his head, her soft feminine moan turning his heart over in his chest and conjuring up all sorts of naughty thoughts. Ones which, if last night was any indication, would be a magnificent mix of sexy and sweet.

He looked down and smiled. She was sprawled across his middle, that soft silky hair of hers spilling over his abs and one long graceful leg draped over his hips. And it took everything he had not to roll her to her back, slide down her beautiful body and coax her awake with his tongue.

Instead, he supported her with his hands, slipped slowly from beneath her then lowered her gently to the mattress. She sighed and shifted to a more comfortable position, settling back into sleep.

A swell of pleasure unfolded in his chest then traveled down his body. Damn, she was beautiful. More beautiful than ever, sleeping in his bed, making love with him. *Loving* him.

He laughed softly, happiness in every fiber of his being. She loved him. Had become his best friend. Lover. And as soon as he could talk her into it, his wife.

The thought made him smile more and he left quietly for the bathroom, fighting the urge to crawl back into bed and make love to her all over again.

He showered and shaved. Dressed, then tugged on his boots. All the while, humming under his breath and making plans.

She'd want an outdoor wedding. He was absolutely sure of that. But would she want to have the ceremony in the afternoon or evening?

He grinned. Evening. A clear night sky filled with the bright stars she'd admired at the overlook.

They're so close, it's like you can touch heaven.

She'd sure felt like heaven in his arms last night, her soft curves cushioning his hard angles and her body wrapping tight around him.

Home had never felt so good.

He grabbed his watch from the dresser, kissed Dani gently on the cheek then lingered by the door, savoring the intoxicating reality of her in his bed. In his life. In his heart.

Fastening his watch around his wrist, Mac winced at the time. Eight fifty-five on a Monday morning. He hadn't slept this late in years and it'd put the routine of early morning work squarely on Cal, Tim and Nate's shoulders. He'd have to haul ass to prepare for the big client scheduled to arrive at nine then hustle to catch up on the chores he'd fallen behind on.

Mac smiled wider. It'd been worth it. He checked on

the children, finding Nadine and Maddie snuggled to-gether, snoring on the unbroken bed. Jaxon was awake. He stood by his bed, still in his pajamas, and rubbed his eyes.

Mac tapped his fingers on the doorframe. Jaxon would make an excellent best man. He and Nate could share the role. "Morning, bud."

He smiled groggily. "Morning."

"Feel like helping me show this bigwig around today?" Mac asked. "He's supposed to be here any minute and I'm running behind. It'd be great if you could help me out."

"Yeah." Jaxon perked up, his eyes becoming more alert, and darted off toward his closet.

"I'll meet you downstairs," Mac said.

He left and stepped briskly down the staircase, whis-tling as he took in the view. The sun shined through the floor-to-ceiling windows and the mist over the mountain range was lighter than usual. The high rocky peaks, colored green with trees and vegetation, rose proudly toward the clear blue sky.

His chest swelled. Elk Valley had never looked so powerful.

The waiting room wasn't overly crowded but it was full. Ann glanced over her shoulder from behind the re-ception desk. She spoke on the phone but smiled when she saw him then motioned toward several couples who were lounging on the new furniture and admiring the view. There were more guests checking in than he could ever recall having seen on a Monday morning.

Busy, she mouthed, excitement in her eyes.

He nodded, laughing softly.

Bright light spilled over the hardwood floor as the

door to the front entrance opened then disappeared as it slammed shut. Nate rounded the reception desk and stopped at the end of the hall just as Mac reached it.

"Sorry, I'm late," Mac said, grinning. "Hope I didn't put you out this morning."

Nate frowned, his expression distant. "What do you mean?"

Mac glanced at his brother's rumpled clothing—the same outfit he'd worn at last night's party—then the rumpled disarray of his hair. "You didn't stay on the ranch last night, did you?"

Nate avoided his eyes, ducking his head and edging past him. "No. I went out for drinks after the party wrapped up." His face flushed and he gestured over his shoulder. "Your guy just pulled in behind me. Limo. Expensive suit. You were right about him having money."

"Nate." Mac studied the hard set of his jaw. "What'd you get up to last night?"

"Nothing." He walked off and ascended the stairs. "Can't talk right now. I gotta clean up then lead a trail ride in half an hour."

Mac rubbed his hand over his forehead. What the hell had Nate gotten himself into now? He rarely came home but when he did, it always seemed like he left behind another mess.

The front door opened again and a man entered. Tall, gray-haired and well-groomed, he was the epitome of the wealthy businessman Mac had imagined.

Mac moved forward, meeting him halfway and holding out his hand. "Mr. Vaughn?"

"Daniel, please." The man smiled, cordial and sincere, then shook his hand. "And you're Mac Tenley, I presume?"

"I am." Mac smiled back. "It's good to have you here."

"Is that him, Dad?"

Jaxon walked around the desk, expression curious as he studied the man at Mac's side.

Mac motioned for him to come closer. "Daniel, this is my son, Jaxon. He's gonna help lead your tour today."

"Nice to meet you, Jaxon." Daniel held his hand out, chuckling when Jaxon shook it vigorously. "I'm honored to have you show me around." He leaned down and whispered, voice teasing. "You can point out all the fun spots that stuffy adults like me haven't noticed."

"Do you like to fish?" Jaxon asked eagerly. "Cuz my Uncle Nate showed me a special fishing hole up at Sugar Falls. We caught a lot of trout there. I can show it to you, if you don't mind walking a ways."

Nodding, Daniel straightened. "Oh, I'd enjoy a good long walk. Especially across a stretch of land as magnificent as this." He gestured toward the mountain range, visible through the windows. "The photographs didn't do this valley justice, Mac."

Mac voiced a silent thanks to Jack Austin. He was the best walking advertisement Elk Valley had ever had. "Jack told me he was spreading the word about Elk Valley but he didn't mention he was passing around pictures, too."

Surprise crossed Daniel's face. "Oh, I didn't get them from Jack." He laughed. "Though he has heaped tons of praise on Elk Valley to anyone willing to listen. One of my agents took photos the last time he came out. I could see how much potential there was here but I expected it would take a lot more effort to overhaul the place. And when I heard how well the ranch was doing again, I had to come see it for myself." He glanced around the waiting room then looked up at the high ceilings. "You've got a gorgeous piece of property here. I'm not surprised that Danielle stayed for so long."

"Danielle?" Mac frowned, eyes scanning the group of guests on the other side of the room. All of them were new and Jack's team was the longest reservation they'd had. He didn't recall a Danielle among them.

Daniel held up a hand, a wry look in his eyes. "Sorry. Dani." A small smile appeared. "She never did take to her given name and avoids it every chance she gets. It's the tomboy in her, I suppose." He glanced back out the large window, nodding toward the valley. "Which makes perfect sense why she fell in love with this place. I knew she would. And I understand now why she was so intent upon closing this deal herself."

A deal?

Daniel. Danielle. *Dani.*

Mac's mouth ran dry as the names tangled in his mind, forming knots. He forced himself to speak. "Tell me… Daniel. What kind of business are you in?"

He faced Mac again, his brow furrowing. "Real estate."

A chill crept into Mac's veins, freezing his blood and forming blocks of ice in his heart. "And what is Dani to you?"

Daniel slid his hands in his pockets slowly. "She's my daughter." He scrutinized Mac's face, confusion darkening his eyes. "And one of my best agents."

Mac turned his head and stared out the window at

the landscape Daniel had just admired. The same one his daughter, Danielle—*Dani*—had complimented.

His eyes traced the high peaks of the mountain range, her voice whispering through his mind.

You told me once that a stranger wouldn't know how to protect these mountains. But I do.

Throat closing, he surveyed the valley where Cal assisted guests in packing their backpacks for a hike and Tim saddled horses for the next trail ride.

If you're willing to take a chance and change, I can turn this place around.

His mouth opened soundlessly on a wave of pain. She'd intentionally deceived him in order to take his land. Every word she'd spoken had been a lie.

He raised his eyes to the sky, his vision blurring.

Ask me what I see.

His eyes burned. He could still feel her hands on him. Taste her on his tongue.

It's like you can touch heaven.

"Dad? Is he talking about our Ms. Dani?"

The wounded tremble in Jaxon's voice made Mac's gut heave. He clamped a hand over his mouth.

Dani. *Danielle.* He'd trusted her. Confided in her. Invited her into Jaxon, Nadine and Maddie's lives. And now...

Rapid footsteps approached from behind then halted abruptly a few feet from him.

Mac dragged his hand from his mouth then looked to his right. There she stood. In the dress she'd worn last night, her long hair mussed, cheeks flushed and mouth still slightly swollen from their passionate kisses.

He called her name. Tested it on his tongue. "Danielle Vaughn."

Her shoulders shook. Her hands twisted at her middle. The truth was right there, reflected in her eyes. And Mac's heart crumbled to pieces.

"I'M SORRY."

Dani winced at the inadequacy of her words. They sounded weak and empty. Just like the lies she'd told. The ones that had multiplied so many times over she could no longer count them.

The idle chatter in the waiting room gradually quieted and the phone rang persistently in the background. Mac stood still, his eyes burning into her. Jaxon, tears brimming in his eyes, looked from her to Mac then back again.

"I'm so sorry." Dani's stomach churned. "Mac—"

"I want you off my property." Mac grabbed Jaxon's arm and led him away.

"Ms. Dani?" Jaxon reached for her as he passed and she moved to take his hand.

"Don't." Mac stepped between them and nudged Jaxon toward the hallway. "Go upstairs, Jaxon."

"But, Dad—"

"Go upstairs and stay there with your sisters."

Jaxon walked slowly around the reception desk then to the hallway, looking back at them with every other step.

Jaw clenching, Mac looked at her father then motioned toward the door. "I believe you know the way out."

He turned on his heel and left, disappearing down the hall into a room on the right.

"Dani, what did you do?"

A familiar wave of humiliation returned at the dis-approving sound of her father's voice. "I lied to him."

"About what?"

"About who I was." She bit the inside of her cheek and lifted her arms helplessly, unsure of which fire to try to put out first. Could this get any worse? "Why are you here?"

He frowned. "Jack Austin called and told me you turned this place around. He said Scott told him about the promotion and Jack thought I should reconsider you for the position." He sighed. "I'm not happy with how you handled this but I have to admit, I'm impressed with the work you've done."

She shook her head. "It wasn't just me. It took all of us. The staff. Cal and Tim. Mac and his childr—" Her chest clenched painfully. "Look, I don't care about im-pressing anyone anymore. That's what got me into this mess to begin with. I lied to you. I lied to Mac. And I lied to myself." She shook her head. "I don't want the promotion and I don't want to work at the company anymore, either." She laughed, the sound harsh even to her own ears. "I don't even want to stay in New York."

"Dani—"

"Dad, please." She headed for the hallway. "I can't do this with you right now."

She left, walking past an open-mouthed Ann whose rapt eyes stayed glued to every step she took.

The door to the room Mac had entered was slightly ajar. Dani nudged it open then stepped inside, shut-ting it behind her.

Mac stood at the window, his hands shoved deep in his pockets and his broad back to her.

"Mac."

His shoulders stiffened. "I asked you to leave."

Dani trembled, her legs feeling as though they might give out beneath her. "I know." She swallowed hard. "And after you hear me out, if you still want me to, I will."

"There's nothing left to say."

"There is." She moved closer and smoothed her dress with shaky fingers. "I'm sorry for lying to you. It means nothing now to say that I was going to tell you the truth...but I really was. And I have been telling you the truth for quite some time now."

"Really?" He faced her, the tight set of his expression and shadowed eyes sending a stab of pain through her. "Which part was true, Danielle?" His mouth twisted. "The part where you made me think you were broke and desperate? That you actually needed a job on a run-down ranch about to be seized by the bank?"

She flinched, tears filling her eyes.

"The part where you let me confide in you then tried to talk me into selling my family's land even when you knew I had no intention of doing so." His tone tightened as he moved closer. "The part where you stood with me on the overlook, claiming you wanted to help—"

"I did want to help."

"—then talked me into changing everything." He clenched his fists. *"Everything."* He winced, his face paling. "Or the part where you lay in my bed? When you put your hands on me and told me you loved me?"

A sob broke past her lips. She ran over, wrapped her arms around his waist and pressed her cheek to his chest. "That wasn't a lie. Nothing about last night was a lie." She squeezed him harder. "I love you, Mac. More than anything."

His arms stayed still by his sides, his voice strained. "I didn't even know your real name until today."

"Mac, please." She lifted her head and cradled his face, her thumbs brushing over the tight clench of his jaw. "I never lied about loving you. When I came here, I pretended to be someone I'm not because I wanted to buy this land and impress my father. But things changed and I fell in love with you." She pressed closer. "The woman who kissed you at Sugar Falls was me. I'm the same woman you went camping with. The one you held in your arms by the creek. And it was me last night, loving you and wanting you more than anything in the world."

He stared down at her, silently.

"I wish there was an easy answer," she whispered. "I wish I could go back and do things differently, but I can't. I wish I could tell you that I wasn't the woman who lied to you. Who gave you a different name and was desperate to be something more than she was. But that was me, too." She lifted to her toes, touched her forehead to his. "I'm not perfect, Mac. I messed up. I did a lot of dumb things trying to earn my father's approval and none of it mattered because love doesn't work that way. Not real love. The kind I feel for you." She brushed her lips against his, kissing him softly. "You know me better than anyone. The real me. Flaws and all. And all I can do is start over, ask you to forgive me and hope that you can."

His eyes squeezed shut and his arms wrapped around her, holding her close. It was quiet for a few moments then he spoke, his voice heavy. "But you didn't just lie to me. You lied to my kids."

Her heart sank and she sagged against him, hot tears rolling down her cheeks. "I know."

His big hands drifted over her hair then smoothed over her shoulders. She hid her face against the base of his throat and cried, memorizing the feel of his strong palms on her skin.

After a while, he released her then walked slowly to the door. He opened it and turned away from her. "Please leave, Dani."

She wrapped her arms around her waist and tried to regain her composure. "C-can I tell them goodbye?"

He looked back at her. His cheeks were wet and a muscle in his jaw clenched. "I don't think that's a good idea. This is going to hurt them enough as it is."

Dani nodded, choking back another sob, then left quietly.

She returned to the cabin, changed her clothes then packed the few items she'd brought with her in her ragged bag. Hitching the worn strap over her shoulder, she took one last look around then started up the dirt path to her car.

"Here." Nate stepped alongside her, his pace slowing to match hers as he lifted the bag from her shoulder. "Let me help you out with that."

She averted her eyes and watched her scuffed shoes move across the dirt with each step. "I guess you heard about what happened."

"Yeah. I ran across your father on my way out and Ann's been telling everyone within a ten-mile radius." He laughed, the sound humorless. "News travels fast around Elk Valley. That's one of the reasons I keep my distance from this place."

"I should've listened to you." She dragged the back of her hand across her wet face. "I should've told Mac myself a long time ago."

"Maybe. But do you really think it would've made a difference?"

She shrugged. "I don't know. But at least he wouldn't have found out from someone else. I could've spared him that."

They reached her car and Nate put her bag in the passenger seat. "Give him some time. He might come around."

Fresh tears surged to her eyes and she turned away. Blinking hard, she focused on the mountains in the distance. The smoky mist was thin and the sun shined bright across the valley.

How in the world would she manage to leave Elk Valley and start over? Without Jaxon, Nadine and Maddie? Without Mac?

Nate gestured across the valley. "There's a couple people that want to speak to you before you go."

She rolled her lips and looked at the fields. Horses were saddled in one of the paddocks and a group of guests sat on the ground by their backpacks.

Tim and Cal noticed her, left the group of guests and strode over to the car.

"Headed out?" Tim asked.

She nodded. "I'm not exactly welcome anymore. I'm sorry I didn't tell you who I really was."

Cal scoffed. "We know exactly who you are."

Dani rubbed her forehead, her stomach churning

with guilt and embarrassment. "Look, Cal. I don't want to argue with you right n—"

"You're a damned hard worker and a helluva good boss."

Her eyes shot to his. There wasn't a trace of sarcasm or mocking in his gaze. Just sincerity and...*admiration*?

Cal tipped his chin to the mountains in the distance. "Not just anyone could come in here and bring this place back to life. You got to understand the land, respect your team and work your ass off. You're damned good at all that."

She gaped then struggled to find her voice. "You... you think I'm a good boss?"

"No." He raised an eyebrow, his lips twitching. "I said you're a helluva good boss. Get it straight, city girl, 'cuz I ain't got time to explain it to you."

Surprisingly, that made her smile. Then laugh. And before she could reconsider it, she threw her arms around Cal and hugged him as tight as she could. "Thank you."

He patted her back awkwardly then wiggled away, a scowl on his face. "You could cut back on the girly stuff though. Ain't got time for this foolishness. There's work to do." He spun and stomped off. "Come on, Tim. We got guests waiting."

Tim smiled and tipped his hat. "It was a pleasure working with you, ma'am."

Heart aching, Dani whispered, "Same here."

Chapter Twelve

Mac nudged a bowl of strawberries across the kitchen table toward Maddie. "Eat up, baby."

She continued pushing scrambled eggs around her plate, her breakfast mostly untouched. "I'm not hungry."

He picked up the bowl and moved it the other side of the table. "Nadine?"

"No, thank you," she said, poking a slice of ham with her fork.

Mac moved it to the left. "Jaxon?"

He looked up from the table briefly, glancing at the strawberries. "Uh-uh."

Sighing, Mac returned the bowl to its original position. In the two weeks since Dani had left, all three of them picked at their food, rarely cracked a smile and barely talked. And he couldn't blame them, since he'd done the same.

As much as he hated to admit it, he missed Dani. Missed her smile and her laugh. Even her sassy ponytail. Nothing on the ranch had been the same since she'd left.

"I got to head out," Nate said, rising from the table and tossing his napkin on his plate. "I need to get on the road if I'm gonna make it to that competition in Texas."

"You can't stay a few more days?" Mac asked.

He'd known it was coming. Nate had been as morose as he and the children had over the past two weeks, though Mac suspected it was for a reason other than Dani leaving. And Nate had grown especially antsy over the last couple of days. A sure sign he was getting ready to bolt again.

"What for?" Nate shook his head. "You canceled the last two reservations we had for retreats and Cal and Tim are handling the hikes and trail rides fine on their own. You don't need an extra hand anymore."

Mac stilled, smiling a little as he recalled the day Dani had arrived. He could still see her standing there with her hands on her hips and fire in her eyes, insisting she could do the job. He'd had his doubts, but she'd proved him wrong and pulled it off—in more ways than he'd suspected at the time.

The thought punched another hole in his heart, a stark reminder of why he'd halted the corporate retreats Ann had booked. It wasn't just the bitter taste in his mouth that had made him throw in the towel. It was also the fact that the new side of Elk Valley Ranch's business just didn't work well without Dani.

Between his lack of drive and business floundering again, he hadn't seen the point. So, he'd neglected to submit the back payment on his loan. Which meant the thick envelope bearing the bank's logo that Cal had brought in this morning more than likely contained a foreclosure notice. Mac hadn't had the courage to open it and face the reality yet.

"Stay at least one more day, Nate," Mac said through stiff lips.

"And do what?" Nate asked. "Sit in the lodge and

stagnate? That's all you've been doing for the past week."

Mac winced. The idea of returning to his regular routine, for however much longer he owned this place, filled him with dread. He'd tried going through the motions for several days after Dani had left but almost every square inch of the ranch reminded him of her.

He could still see her swinging that ax in the field, a satisfied expression on her face. Could still feel her soft lips against his as he rode his horse past the paddock fence she'd helped repair. And he swore he could still smell her sweet scent in his bed despite the fact that he'd changed the sheets at least a dozen times.

"We could all hike up to the overlook," Mac added. "Camp out for a night or two."

That'd get him away from the ranch for a little while, at least. But the problem was, the memories of Dani's soft touch and open arms didn't exist solely in his bed or on the land. They were rooted firmly in his heart.

"You hear that, kids?" Nate leaned on the table and smiled. "Your dad wants to know if you want to hike up to the overlook and camp. Want to go?"

Jaxon crossed his arms, Maddie shook her head and Nadine stabbed the ham on her plate harder, rattling the dishes on the table.

Nate looked at Mac and raised his brows. "There's your answer."

Mac dragged a hand across the back of his neck. "Jaxon, take the dirty dishes to the sink, please."

"If I do, can I call Ms. Dani?"

Maddie straightened in her chair and blinked. Nadine stilled, her fork sticking in the mutilated meat.

"Jaxon, take the dishes—"

"That's not an answer." He shoved away from the table and stood. "Can I call her or not?"

Mac stiffened. "I know you're upset, son, but you need to watch your tone. Don't raise your voice to me."

Jaxon blushed and dipped his head. "Yes, sir. I'm sorry," he mumbled. "I just miss her."

"Me, too," Maddie said.

"Why can't we call her, Dad?" Nadine asked.

Mac cringed. "Because things are complicated."

"What kind of complicated?" Nadine asked.

Mac hesitated. After Dani had left, he hadn't had the courage to explain the entire situation to the girls. He'd told them as gently as he could that Dani had returned to New York for another job. It hadn't been the whole truth, but it was the best he could manage at the time.

Jaxon, on the other hand, had seen and heard the majority of what had happened and his resentment at being unable to reach out to Dani grew more intense with each of Mac's refusals.

"She said she was sorry." Jaxon frowned, his mouth trembling. "Why won't you just give her a chance to fix it?"

"Fix what?" Nadine asked.

Mac rubbed his temples. "She lied, Jaxon. To all of us."

"People make mistakes," Nate said quietly.

Mac shot his brother a look. "You're not helping, Nate."

Nate shrugged and held up his hands.

"What did Ms. Dani lie about?" Maddie asked.

Mac glanced at Maddie. She looked up at him, confused and vulnerable, and he had no idea how to explain it to her. "Ms. Dani lied about why she came here. She's not a ranch hand and she didn't need the work."

Nadine scooted close to his side. "But did she say she was sorry?"

Mac grimaced. "Nadine—"

"Yes," Jaxon said firmly. "She did say she was sorry. Didn't she, Dad?"

Mac shifted in his seat and rubbed his chin. "She did but—"

"No buts." Nadine pointed her finger at him and shook it. "If she said she's sorry then everything's okay."

Mac groaned. "Nadine, that's not how it works."

"Yes, it is." She rose to her knees in her chair and brought her face level to his. "When I make Maddie cry, someone always make me say I'm sorry then everything's okay. That's how it works."

Mac smiled and brushed his fingers through her hair. "That's true. But this is different."

"Why's it different?" Nadine asked.

"It's different because Ms. Dani did something that hurt us all very badly."

Maddie climbed up close to him, too, and frowned. "So you don't love her anymore?"

Mac froze. His heart gave a clear answer but his head didn't want to acknowledge it.

"Because you said…" Maddie's brow furrowed and she thought for a minute before reciting, "You said, if you love someone, there's nothing they can do or not do to make you love them any less." She stared at him, expression earnest. "That's what you told me. Was that true, too?"

God help me. Mac slumped back in his seat, study-ing the accusation in his daughters' eyes. He was at a loss—*a complete damned loss*—of how to argue his point.

Nadine looked at Maddie, nodded then climbed down from her chair. "Maybe *you* need to say you're sorry, Dad." She stacked her dirty dishes then glanced at him with a stern expression. "And make it a polite one, 'cuz that's the kind Ms. Dani likes."

She sashayed to the sink, dumped her dirty dishes in it then left, saying over her shoulder, "I'm going out to play."

Maddie and Jaxon smiled then followed suit, put-ting away their dirty dishes and chasing each other out of the room.

Nate laughed and rocked back on his heels. "Just so you know, that kid got her smarts from me, not you."

Mac grunted. "I wouldn't go that far."

"It's true," Nate said, voice firming. "Otherwise, you'd be talking things out with Dani right now in-stead of trying to defend yourself to your seven-year-old daughter."

Mac's cheeks heated. "You know this isn't that sim-ple."

"In this situation? With you and Dani?" Nate nod-ded. "Yeah, it is. You may not have had a choice with Nicole all those years ago, but you've got one right now with Dani."

"And what choice would that be?"

"You can choose to forgive her." Nate dragged a hand over his face. "Not all of us do the right thing like you. Some of us screw things up pretty badly. I know I do."

Mac sat silently, studying his brother.

"It's your choice, Mac. Think of what your life would be like without her."

Soon after, Nate packed his bags, hugged the kids and drove away. Mac watched the truck rumble down the long driveway and disappear over the hill.

He glanced around the valley. He looked at the mountains then watched as Cal returned from a trail ride, a group of guests following him on horseback across the green field. Then he looked over his shoulder at the lodge, studying the wide windows and high roof. Elk Valley Ranch was, as Daniel Vaughn had put it, a gorgeous piece of property.

But was it more valuable than Dani?

Laughter rang out and Mac turned his attention to the paddock, smiling as Jaxon, Nadine and Maddie chased each other. He closed his eyes and revisited what he used to see. He pictured his children in the future but, this time, imagined his family somewhere else. Somewhere with Dani.

Ask me what I feel.

Mac opened his eyes and laughed, his heart growing so big he thought his chest would burst. It didn't matter if he lost Elk Valley Ranch. It didn't matter where he lived or what he owned. Home wasn't in the lodge or on the mountain. It was right there in his children's laughter. In Dani's arms. And he couldn't imagine his life without her.

He jogged back inside, went to his office and grabbed the letter from the bank. No longer afraid of the bad news, he opened the envelope, pulled the paper out and unfolded it. But the document in his hand wasn't a foreclosure notice. Instead, it was a deed.

It took Mac three phone calls to discover who'd made the payment. He smiled then dialed another number.

"Vaughn Real Estate. How may I direct your call?"

DANI OPENED THE last unemptied drawer of her desk and sifted through the items inside.

"Hope there's not a lot in that one you want to keep." Scott placed a small box on top of the desk in front of her and grinned. "This is the last sturdy box we have and it's barely big enough for two packs of printer paper."

She glanced around her office, the third biggest in the Vaughn Real Estate building, and frowned at the dozen or so taped boxes filled with books, papers and knickknacks—none of which she really needed. They were just nostalgic pieces of a former career she no longer wanted.

Smiling, she plucked a pad of sticky notes from the bottom of the drawer then tossed it in the box. "There."

He laughed. "Seriously?"

She reached back and adjusted her ponytail. "Seriously. Those will be perfect for recording my new life goals. The rest of this stuff I can't really use where I'm going."

"And where might that be?"

Dani glanced up. Her father stood in the doorway, sporting a custom-made suit and stern expression.

"I'm not sure yet," she said. "Some place green and spacious with lots of fresh air." She smirked. "And cheap. It will definitely have to be cheap now that I'm broke."

He entered the office, motioning toward the door. "Would you give us a moment alone, Scott?"

"Of course." Scott left, smiling sympathetically over his shoulder.

"You still have the option of changing your mind, you know?" Her father nudged one of the boxes on the floor with the toe of his polished shoe. "Your old job is still available. A better one, too, if you want it."

Dani drummed her fingers on the glass top of her desk. "A step up?"

"Several."

She smiled. "Sounds tempting. But I'll pass."

"I thought as much."

Her smile faded. "Did you?"

"I know you better than you think I do, Dani."

Averting her eyes, she pushed the desk drawer closed. "Sometimes it doesn't feel that way."

"That's my fault."

Her hand stilled on the drawer handle and she glanced at him in surprise.

"Do you know why I gave the promotion to Scott?"

She straightened, shoving her hands in her pockets. "Because you had more faith in him."

"No." He walked to her side, wincing as he spoke. "I gave Scott the position because I honestly couldn't picture you still working here in fifteen or twenty years."

Dani stared, heat sweeping over her skin. "What did you say?"

"I considered it." He hesitated, spreading his hands. "I tried to convince myself that you'd stay. That you'd fall in love with the job at some point and decide to make this a life-long career. But I just couldn't see that happening."

She shook her head slightly. "You...you couldn't see it?"

"No." He laughed. "Honestly, every time I thought about where you'd be in twenty years, all I could see was you hiking the Pacific Crest Trail, kayaking the Colorado River or cycling a Chicago bikeway." He shrugged, voice faltering. "I tried to imagine you sitting in this office. Signing documents and negotiating prices. It just didn't feel right."

Dani's chest tingled and the feeling spread, fluttering inside her. "You thought about where I'd be in twenty years? Imagined it?"

"I realize I'm probably way off base..." He smoothed his tie and looked away, his cheeks flushing. "But just out of curiosity, could you ever see yourself doing any of those things?"

She smiled. "Yes. At least the hiking part."

Her heart skipped a beat at the thought of hiking with Mac to the overlook. The memory of sitting by the creek with him as he described the futures he hoped for Maddie, Nadine and Jaxon. There'd been such pride and admiration in his voice. The kind only a father who loved his child would have.

The kind that filled her father's voice now.

"That's what I pictured the most." A pleased sigh left him and he smiled. "Mountains and trees. Fresh air and sunshine. Some place like Elk Valley."

She pulled in a swift breath, her chest tightening.

"The photos of that place..." He laughed softly. "I could just see you there. Clear as day. That's why I was so intent upon acquiring it. We knew it was a potential money-maker but I also knew when we did begin transforming the place, you'd be the perfect one to oversee the process. And I hoped—"

"You hoped I'd take a position there," Dani said, heart pounding hard in her chest.

"Yes. I hoped you'd be happy there. Happier than you were here." He lifted his hand, tucking a wayward strand of her hair behind her ear and adding gently, "And I thought if we owned it, even with you all those miles away, you'd still be home."

Tears spilled over her lashes, tickling her cheeks. "I was."

He kissed the top of her head. "Maybe you will be again."

Dani forced a small smile. "No. It belongs to the right person now." She scrubbed the back of her hand over her cheeks and laughed. "But you're welcome to visit my tent on the Pacific Crest Trail as soon as I get settled. A sleeping bag and stars might be the perfect fit for a while."

He hugged her then headed for the door, stopping at the threshold. "I took the liberty of arranging for a few people to help you move your things. If you're all done here, I can send them up now, if you'd like?"

"That'd be great, thanks. And, Dad?" She swallowed hard as he looked back at her. "I love you."

He smiled. "I love you, too, Dani."

After he left, she walked to the windows lining her office wall and looked down. The New York streets looked small from the forty-fifth floor and the tall buildings surrounding her father's obscured the view of the horizon.

She pressed her forehead to the cool glass then closed her eyes, imagining herself back at Elk Valley

Ranch's overlook. She pictured the birds floating on the breeze, conjured up the powerful mountain peaks and willed that warm comforting sensation back into her veins. The one she felt when Mac wrapped his arms around her and held her close.

She held on to each image—each feeling—as tightly as she could, knowing she would probably never have them again.

"See something you like out there?"

Startled, she jumped. Her head thumped against the window and her hands squeaked across the pristine glass as she spun around.

Mac stood by her desk, a slow smile spreading across his face as he gestured toward the window. "I got to admit, it's an interesting place. A little loud for my tastes but I could get used to it."

Her eyes, hungry for the sight of him, moved slowly down his muscular length. His broad shoulders and wide chest were encased in a T-shirt and his jeans clung snugly to his lean hips and thick thighs.

She opened and closed her mouth soundlessly, unable to find her voice.

He smiled wider.

"Told you they had four elevators." Nadine walked in, Maddie and Jaxon hot on her heels.

Jaxon scoffed. "You didn't know 'til you saw them."

"She did so kno—" Maddie halted abruptly then ran over, shouting, "Ms. Dani!"

She barreled into Dani's middle and wrapped her arms around her legs. Jaxon and Nadine, all smiles, ran over and did the same, causing Dani to stumble backward against the window.

Dani laughed as she bent and struggled to hug

them all back at once. "I... Why are you all... How did you..."

She shook her head, happy tears filling her eyes, and kissed the tops of their heads.

Nadine looked up, her chin poking into Dani's belly. "We flew on a plane."

"A jet," Jaxon corrected. He smiled. "Your Dad's."

"It had a TV and a bed," Maddie said, bouncing against Dani's leg. "And we could see the whole world from up there."

"From here, too." Nadine released Dani and scooted over to the window, pressing her face against the glass and looking down. "Come look."

Mac chuckled. "Kids."

Dani smiled as all three of them swiveled around and looked up at him.

He raised an eyebrow, giving them a knowing look. "You mind waiting outside for a minute?"

"Why?" Maddie asked.

Nadine elbowed her. "You know why." She smiled, skipping toward the door. "Come on."

Jaxon and Maddie hugged Dani once more then left.

Nadine paused at the door, cupped her hands around her mouth and whispered loudly to Mac. "If you get stuck, just come get me and I'll help you get it right."

Confused, Dani watched her leave then turned to Mac. "What are you supposed to be getting right?"

He smiled. "My apology."

"For what?"

His eyes roved over her then returned to her face. "For being hardheaded and letting the woman I love slip through my fingers."

Her breath caught and she stared at him wordlessly.

"I received a deed for the ranch yesterday." He walked over to the window and stood beside her. "Any idea who made that happen?"

She nodded.

"Seems to me, you'll be needing a job now," he said. "Probably a place to stay, too, seeing as how you quit your job and sold your share in your father's company to pay off Elk Valley Ranch's debt."

"How did you find out?"

"I called your father."

"There are no strings with that, Mac," she whispered. "You don't owe me anything."

"I know." He hooked his finger into the front pocket of her jeans and tugged her close. "But there's a position at the ranch I think you might be interested in." He lowered his head, his lips brushing against her ear. "And you're the only one qualified for it."

She nuzzled his cheek, his familiar scent and soothing tone making her melt against him. "Mac—"

"Close your eyes," he said softly, shutting his then kissing her lashes gently.

Her eyelids fluttered shut and she pressed her hands to his chest. "But—"

"Ask me what I see."

She stilled, feeling his warm forehead press to hers and his big palms cup her face. "What do you see?"

"Us. Dozens of years from now. Standing on the overlook under a million stars." His hands slid down, caressing her shoulders. "I hear us telling each other how happy we are. How amazing it is that we're even more in love than we were all those years ago, standing right here. And how that love keeps growing stronger every day." He slid his hands over her back, pulling her closer. "I hear Maddie and Nadine asking you for advice on how to be a good mom because they want their children to feel as loved by them as they did by you. And I hear Jaxon asking me how to find the courage to propose to the woman he loves." His hands left her, his arms brushing hers as he moved. "Because he's seen how happy we've been over the years and he knows it all started right here."

He lifted her hand from his chest and placed something in her palm.

Dani opened her eyes and smiled, tears spilling down her cheeks as she looked at the diamond ring in her hand.

"Now, ask me what I feel," he whispered, green eyes staring into hers.

She lifted to her toes, brushing her lips over his, then asked, "What do you feel?"

"Loved." He smiled then blew out a heavy breath. "And scared to damn death that you might say no."

She laughed and threw her arms around his neck.

He hugged her, squeezing her tight and whispering, "I love you, Dani."

"I love you, too."

"Is that a yes?"

"Yes."

Mac kissed her, slowly and tenderly, and Dani knew she'd found home right there in his arms.

* * * * *

If you loved this novel, don't miss
April Arrington's previous books in her
MEN OF RAINTREE RANCH *series:*

TWINS FOR THE BULL RIDER
THE RANCHER'S WIFE
THE BULL RIDER'S COWGIRL
THE RANCHER'S MIRACLE BABY

Available now from Harlequin Western Romance!

We hope you enjoyed this story from
Harlequin® Western Romance.

Harlequin® Western Romance is coming to an end, but community, cowboys and true love are here to stay. Starting July 2018, discover more heartfelt tales of family and friendship from **Harlequin® Special Edition**.

Romance is for life, and these stories show that every chapter in a relationship has its challenges and delights and that love can be renewed with each turn of the page!

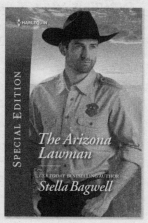

Look for six *new* romances every month from **Harlequin® Special Edition!**
Available wherever books are sold.

Get 2 Free Books,
Plus 2 Free Gifts—
just for trying the Reader Service!

SPECIAL EXCERPT FROM

⊕ HARLEQUIN®

Western Romance

*Could Bridgett Monroe's shocking discovery soften the
notoriously rigid Cullen McCabe?*

Read on for a sneak preview of
THE TEXAS COWBOY'S BABY RESCUE,
the first book in Cathy Gillen Thacker's series
TEXAS LEGENDS: THE MCCABES.

Cullen McCabe slammed to a halt just short of her.

His dark brows lowered like thunderclouds over
mesmerizing blue eyes. Her breath caught in her chest.

"Is this an April Fool's joke?" he demanded gruffly.

Suddenly feeling angry, Bridgett gestured at the sleeping
infant beyond the nursery's glass window. The adorable
newborn had curly espresso brown hair and gorgeous blue
eyes.

Just like the man in front of her.

"Does this look like a joke, McCabe?" Because it sure
wasn't to Bridgett, who'd found the abandoned baby.

Their eyes clashed, held for an interminably long
moment. Cullen looked back, lingering on the tag attached
to the infant bed: Robby Reid McCabe.

"What do I have to do with this baby? Other than that we
apparently share the same last name?"

Bridgett reached into the pocket of her scrubs and
withdrew the rumpled envelope. "This was left beside the
fire station along with the child."

With a scowl, he opened the envelope, pulled out the
typewritten paper and read out loud, "Cullen, I know

you never planned to have a family or get married, and I understand that, but please be the daddy little Robby deserves."

Reacting like he'd landed on some crazy reality TV show, Cullen looked around suspiciously.

To no avail. The only cameras were the security ones the hospital employed. As Cullen stepped closer to the glass and gave the baby another intent look, Bridgett inched nearer and stared up at him. At six foot four, he towered over her.

"You found him?"

She nodded.

Cullen's expression radiated compassion. "I'm sorry to hear that." His voice dropped. "But unfortunately, I don't have any connection to this baby."

"Sure about that?"

He frowned at her. "Think I'd know if I'd conceived a child with someone."

"Not necessarily," she countered. Not if he hadn't been told.

Briefly, a deep resentment seemed to flicker in his gaze.

He lowered his face to hers and spoke in a masculine tone that sent a thrill down her spine. "I'd know if I'd slept with someone in the last ten months or so."

He paused to let that sink in. "Obviously, you don't believe me."

Bridgett shrugged. "It's not up to me to believe you or not." This was becoming too personal, too fast.

Don't miss THE TEXAS COWBOY'S BABY RESCUE by Cathy Gillen Thacker, available April 2018 wherever Harlequin® Western Romance books and ebooks are sold.

www.Harlequin.com